# And 1

## Sherri Vollbracht Fuchs

PublishAmerica
Baltimore

© 2003 by Sherri Vollbracht Fuchs.

All rights reserved. No part of this book may be reproduced, stored in a retrieval system or transmitted in any form or by any means without the prior written permission of the publishers, except by a reviewer who may quote brief passages in a review to be printed in a newspaper, magazine or journal.

First printing

ISBN: 1-4137-0516-2
PUBLISHED BY PUBLISHAMERICA, LLLP
www.publishamerica.com
Baltimore

Printed in the United States of America

*For my family and in loving memory of my grandma, Alice, who lived in Cincinnati during the influenza epidemic of 1918*

# Chapter One

Alice carefully painted P A U L in red over the black and white newsprint and dropped her paintbrush into a water-filled tin can. She blew on the hat-sized triangle of newspaper. The wet paint glistened in the bright sunlight streaming in the kitchen windows. Impatiently she waved her hands over the scarlet lettering and blew again.

"Be careful, Alice!" Ellen cried, snatching a cake she had frosted out of Alice's reach. "You almost knocked Paul's cake right off the table."

"I did not," Alice replied between blows. Ellen thought she knew everything just because she was sixteen and Alice was only fourteen.

"You did too. And why are you wasting time on that silly hat? Mama told you to help me with the meal. She won't get home till just before Paul arrives." Ellen smoothed back a stray wisp of honey brown hair and wiped the sweat from her brow.

"In a minute," Alice said. "I'm almost done."

She gave the hat a final blow, slipped her fingers into the opening on the long end of the triangle and plopped the hat onto her own head. Darting for the dining room mirror, she almost knocked over the red jar of paint.

"Alice! Be careful!" Ellen's words followed Alice into the next room where she wove around the polished table and slid to a stop in front of the oval mirror hanging over the sideboard.

The hat flattened her walnut hair against her cheeks and covered one large brown eye. "Happy 18th Birthday Paul!" the red paint proclaimed over the top of last week's news. Tiny rivulets of wet paint from the 'P' in Paul dripped into the bold newsprint announcing *The Cincinnati Post* and the tiny date, August 31, 1918. The headline read *Wilson Calls on Men 18-45 to Register on September 12.*

Alice had tried to cover up President Wilson's words with her bright lettering. What awful words to have on a birthday hat. But every page of the newspaper was filled with awful words. War, war, war. *Buy War Bonds. Support the War Effort. Four More Local Boys Die in Combat.*

Each evening after Mama, Ellen, and Alice did the dishes, the family gathered back around the table and Father read the paper aloud. Father's deep, calm voice filled the room. The gas lamps hanging on the walls and over the table created soft pools of light. The stories of foreign sounding battles and thousands of casualties seemed like made-up fairytales gone horribly wrong.

Why were people attacking and killing each other? Alice wondered if the fighting would reach American soil. Would German armies march through the streets of Cincinnati killing people just because they were Americans? She shuddered.

"Alice, will you please come help me?" Ellen called impatiently from the kitchen.

"Coming," Alice replied. She took one last look at the hat in the mirror, slipped it off and placed it neatly over Paul's plate. The table looked beautiful, set for seven people with the good china and silverware. The white lace tablecloth tatted by Grandma Brockmann covered the oak table and white linen napkins, each embroidered with a navy 'B,' lay in neat triangles at each place.

Gentle, cheerful Grandma Brockmann had died last year of tuberculosis and the whole family missed her terribly, especially Grandpa. Her piano now stood proudly in the parlor, its tinkling notes forever happy reminders of her. Grandpa still had moments of quiet sadness, but he was back to his old self most of the time. He'd be here for the birthday celebration.

Mama was likely helping him up the streetcar steps at this moment, after her long day volunteering for the Red Cross. Grandpa was probably grumbling and complaining. "In my day, horses or our own two legs were good enough for anybody. Don't see the use in these newfangled contraptions." Grandpa's gravely voice rattled in Alice's memory and she smiled. Grandpa had an opinion about everything: from the war to raising chickens to trolley-cars. He was stubborn as a mule, but Alice loved him.

Ellen came to the kitchen door, face flushed, baked potatoes in a cloth in her arms. Steam rose from the potatoes and from Ellen. Alice stopped smiling, adjusted the fork at Paul's place and hurried to her

sister's aid. "Sorry," she mumbled.
The girls made final preparations for dinner. Ellen worked smoothly and efficiently. Alice worked quickly. As she rushed to fill a blue ceramic bowl with fresh baked rolls, Alice's elbow bumped the baked potatoes piled neatly on the stove to keep warm.

"Ouch," she cried, grabbing her burnt elbow as the potatoes tumbled over the edge of the black cast-iron stove and thumped one after another onto the wooded floor. She snatched the last one triumphantly before it hit the floor, then quickly dropped it as it burnt her fingers.

"Ouch!" Alice blew on her stinging fingertips.

"Alice! What are you doing?" Ellen stopped slicing meatloaf to rescue the potatoes, her blue satin dress brushing the floor. Alice grabbed a dishcloth and stooped to help.

"Sorry," Alice said. In the stuffy kitchen sweat poured off Alice's forehead, landing in dark droplets on her peach dress.

"I know you didn't mean to, but you need to be more careful. Mama put us in charge of Paul's dinner and I want it to turn out nice."

"Mama put *you* in charge of dinner. She knew I'd ruin it."

"You know perfectly well how to get dinner on. But your mind wanders or you go too fast and things fall apart."

"Or fall on the floor." Alice smiled, trying to lighten the moment. Ellen picked up the last potato and wearily smiled back.

"Why don't you get Ben and make sure he's cleaned up and ready. I'll finish here."

"I'm sure he's clean. He's the cleanest six-year-old in America." Alice tossed her dishcloth on the table and slipped out the back door to find her brother.

The cool breeze refreshed her after the sweltering heat of the kitchen. An early morning shower made the yard smell of damp earth and foliage. A large, rectangular war garden stretched green and lush toward the creek at the back of the yard, thanks to bucket after bucket of water dragged from the creek all summer.

Alice walked through the carefully tended garden, running the silky tassels of corn through her fingers, and popping a sweet pea pod into her mouth. Alice knew that under the dark earth there were potatoes waiting to be dug up along with carrots and beats. Due to the war, her family grew more in the garden than they had when she was little. If each family did their part to feed themselves, more food was available to send to the army training camps and troops overseas.

Passing the broccoli on the edge of the garden, Alice reached the back of the yard where large trees skirted the trickling creek. The shallow water gurgled and danced. Alice found Ben sitting on the large smooth rock in the middle of the creek. With a long stick he was poking at something in the water. His knickers were pulled up high on each leg to keep them dry and his shoes were lined up side by side next to him on the rock. Alice knew his socks were neatly folded inside each shoe.

"Whatcha doing, Ben?" Alice asked, plopping down in the cool damp grass under her maple tree, her private thinking, dreaming tree.

"Watching the crawdads," Ben replied. He looked up briefly then returned his gaze to the water and his stick.

"Did you find any big ones?"

"Naw, just little ones. Is Paul home?"

"Nope, and neither are the grown-ups. But they should be here any minute. You're supposed to get ready."

"Okay." Ben stood and collected his shoes. With stick and shoes in one arm and his other arm stretched out for balance he slowly stepped and hopped from one stone to the next until he reached the bank. He brushed off a rock next to Alice and sat down.

Ben slipped on his socks, pulled them up to meet his knickers, and tugged them until they were just right. Next he pulled on his black shiny shoes. He meticulously twisted and looped the shoestrings with his stubby six-year-old fingers until the right shoe had an almost perfect bow. Then he started on the left shoe.

Alice groaned. How could shoe tying take this long? When Alice was six she would have walked right into the creek with her shoes on and let them dry as she ran around the yard or climbed her tree. She may have done that now, at fourteen, even though she knew better.

As Ben untied the left shoestring for a third time, Alice stood. Making sure Ben was still concentrating on his laces, she cautiously stretched her arm into the branches of her tree. Standing on her tiptoes, she felt…around…until…there it was. The secret crevice. Her fingertips brushed against something smooth hidden in the rough split in the tree. She smiled. A note from Alex! She'd have to sneak out later and read it.

"Whatcha doin'?"

Alice jolted, scratching her skin on the bark as she hurriedly brought her hand back to her side. Ben stared at her, shoes tied.

"Nothing," she said.

"Didn't look like nothin'."

"What does nothing look like?"

"Huh?" Ben gawked at Alice, shrugged, and took another look at his shoes. Licking his finger, he rubbed at a minute spot of dirt.

Alice sighed and wondered how she'd lived this long without going crazy. She had a nosy little brother who stayed neat as a newly made bed, had his nose in a book half the day, and did everything in slow motion. And he was a tattletale—going to Mama or Ellen to report Alice's every activity.

Ellen was another problem. Miss Perfect, always busy, doing what she was told, getting perfect grades, looking beautiful without seeming to notice. Alice was sick of being compared to Ellen every second of the day.

Paul was the only reason she hadn't gone crazy. Paul understood her. He loved to joke, talk, and have adventures. Alice and Paul were two peas in a pod—that's what Father always said.

"Alice, Ben?" Ellen called from the house. "They're here."

"Coming!" Alice turned to Ben. "Ready?"

"I guess so." He pulled the left bow tighter and stood.

"Race you!" Alice said. "I'll give you a head start."

"Naw, you go ahead. I don't wanna get dirty."

Alice shook her head. She raced through the grass, up the steps, and into the stuffy kitchen.

Ellen was draining the broccoli. Mama, arranging meatloaf slices on a china platter, paused to give Alice a kiss on the cheek. Her sweet lilac scent mingled with the spicy kitchen smells.

"You're warm, dear. Are you getting sick?"

"No, Mama, just running."

"I should have known, but I worry with this influenza going around."

"It's not going around here, Mama," Alice said impatiently.

"Not yet, but you can never be too sure. Where's Benjamin?"

"He's coming." Ben came in the back door, smiling as he saw

Mama.

Mama gave him a big hug, tousled his hair, then smoothed it down for him again. "How's my boy?"

"Good, Mama. Is Paul here?"

"Not yet. Soon. Go say 'hi' to your grandfather."

Ben left for the parlor. Alice followed. "Only stay a moment, Alice. I need you in the kitchen."

Alice hurried into the parlor, passing Ben in the dining room. Father, home earlier than usual, sat on the piano bench allowing Grandpa to use his stuffed armchair. The sweet smell of pipe tobacco filled her nose as she gave Grandpa a big hug.

"Hold it there. Are ya trying to squeeze the life out of me?" He laughed gruffly as he patted Alice's back.

"Hi, Grandpa! How was your trip over here?"

"Those newfangled trolley-cars will be the death of me yet. Some fool in front of me had his window wide open like it's the Fourth of July. I thought my hair'd blow right off my head. 'Bout near froze my ears off too."

"It's not that cold out today, Grandpa," Alice said, smiling. "It's September, not December."

"Don't be telling an old man how cold it is. My bones say it's cold. Anyway, I told that whippersnapper to close the window and ya know what he did?"

"What, Grandpa?" Alice and Ben asked together.

"Nothin'. He plain ignored me. Me, his elder. What's this world comin' to?"

"Don't know, Grandpa," Alice said.

"Now let me get at this little one. Come here, Benny. Haven't got my hug from you yet."

Ben walked tentatively over to his grandfather. The old man gave him a squeeze, tousled his hair, and left it standing every which way.

"Grandpa," Ben complained.

"I know, I know. I mussed your hair. Ain't natural for a boy to be too concerned about his looks. You trying to look spiffy for a gal?"

Ben turned radish-red. "No, Grandpa. I just want to look nice for Paul's party."

"You look right nice to me, boy." Grandpa spit into his hand. "Want me to spit shine it for ya?"

Ben looked horrified. He squirmed out of Grandpa's reach and stood behind Alice. The room erupted in laughter.

Alice turned to find Paul, laughing in the front doorway.

"Paul!" she cried, running to him. "Happy birthday!" She gave him a big hug, which he returned with strong arms.

"Thanks, Ally."

"Wait till you see the present I made you! It's a surprise."

Ben piped up, "I have a surprise too."

Paul scooped his little brother up in his arms. "My surprise first!"

"A surprise for me?" Ben asked.

"For all of you." He called toward the kitchen. "Mama, Ellen, come here a minute."

Ellen walked demurely into the room smiling pleasantly, followed by Mama drying a colander on a dishcloth. "What is it dear?" Mama asked.

Alice asked excitedly, "What's the surprise, Paul?"

# Chapter Two

"I've signed up. You're looking at the newest soldier in the United States Army!" Paul announced proudly.

The unreal words leaped from the newspaper headlines on Paul's hat and crashed into Alice's world. The colander Mama had been drying slipped from her dishtowel and clattered onto the floor. Time momentarily stopped. Alice stared at her smiling brother in disbelief, then at her shocked family. Ellen's hands covered her pale cheeks. Ben's eyes were as big as saucers. Even Father and Grandpa looked stunned.

Time zoomed into place again.

"Noooooo!" The word filled Alice's throat, the room, the house, the neighborhood. Her head nearly exploded with the word. Finally her lungs ran out of air and silence rushed in, replacing the scream. Alice darted past her brother, jumped the porch steps, and flew into the street, narrowly avoiding a bicyclist. She stopped. Lifting her hands to the sky she yelled again, "Noooooo!"

"Ally, Ally!" Paul called gently as he clambered down the porch steps and into the brick street. He reached for her arm. Alice jerked her sleeve away and ran—around their house, through their yard, past the war garden. She barely broke stride as she scaled the maple tree next to the creek. Her maple tree.

Her heart pounded and her breathing came in gasps. Then, as her breaths slowed, the tears came. Tears of anger and fear. They blurred the branches and leaves enfolding her. She scrunched herself into a familiar crevice between two limbs and hugged her knees to her chest.

"Sit like a lady." An old echo of Ellen's voice rang in Alice's ears.

"Mind your own business," she told the air and laid her damp cheek on her knees.

Time passed—seconds? minutes? hours?—Alice didn't know or care. As she brushed away a stream of tears, her swollen eyes caught a smear of white amidst the blurred tree branches. Alex's note.

She tugged the paper from its hiding place and read: "Hello, Alice! Give Paul birthday wishes from me. You'll probably be busy celebrating so I won't see you till tomorrow! Alex."

Alice stuffed the letter into her pocket. Celebrating—ha! Paul had ruined that. He was leaving. Leaving to get shot and killed by the Germans. How could he do that to her? Desert her? They were two peas in a pod. Mama had dependable, loving Father; Ellen had tidy, obedient Ben; and Alice had Paul, fun-loving, understanding Paul.

Paul who listened to her complaints when Ellen got too bossy; who helped her with Miss Lang's impossible English essays; who took her on trolley-car rides to anywhere and nowhere and kept her laughing the whole time. Now everything was ruined. Paul was leaving, probably forever.

She felt someone or something squeeze her shoe. Looking down through swollen eyes she met Paul's concerned gaze.

"May I come up?" he asked quietly.

Alice kicked at his hand. "Go away! That's what you want to do anyway, so just leave me alone."

"Ally, I want to talk to you."

"It's a free country. Talk."

"I'm coming up." He selected a branch far from Alice's dangerous feet and easily hoisted his body into the branches. He maneuvered around twigs and limbs until he was resting on the branch next to Alice's crook.

Alice thrust her head back to her knees and stared at the grass far below.

"Come on, Ally, talk to me."

Silence.

"At least look at me."

Alice turned and glared at her big-brother. If looks could kill he wouldn't have to go to Europe to be shot dead by a bunch of Germans. He'd be dead already.

"Better watch out—your face will freeze that way," Paul joked.

Alice ignored him.

"Come on, Ally, you have to talk to me sometime."

"Oh really? Fine, I'll talk. Why are you such a blockhead?"

"Why am I a blockhead just because I want to save our country from the Germans?"

Alice replied, "There's plenty of soldiers fighting the Germans. Father reads about them in the paper every day—getting shot and killed. Why do you have to join them? What's one more soldier to the army?"

"If everyone had that attitude no one would be defending our country," Paul said.

"And the paper wouldn't be filled with deaths and battles."

"You're right. It would be filled with news about Germany taking over Europe, then Asia, then America."

"Well, at least you'd be home with me instead of thousands of miles away."

"That's ridiculous and you know it."

"You could have warned me ahead of time. You're supposed to tell me everything. Lately you don't tell me anything. You probably tell all your secrets to Vivien." Alice rolled her eyes, puckered up her lips, and kissed the air twice.

"Stop that, Ally. Vivien and I are just friends…like you and Alex."

"I saw you kissing on the porch," Alice blurted.

"You shouldn't have been watching. Would you like it if I spied on you and Alex?"

"Go ahead. You wouldn't see anything. Alex and I are just friends." They'd been friends for about six years, since the night Ben was born. Alice glared a warning at Paul, her cheeks felt red-hot.

Paul put his hands up in surrender. "If you say so. Anyway, Vivien doesn't know I signed up. I didn't tell her yet. And I didn't tell you ahead of time because I knew you'd get mad."

"You were right!" Alice uncurled like an angry snake and shoved her brother with all her furious, frustrated strength.

Paul grasped for a twig. It snapped in his hand. He frantically grabbed at a branch as he tumbled out of the tree. Arms flailing he landed with a sickening thud on the earth below.

Alice stared shocked for a second, then scrambled down the tree to her beloved brother. He lay still.

"Paul! Paul! Are you okay? I'm sorry! I didn't mean it!" She cradled her brother's head in her lap and stroked his hair. "Please wake up, Paul."

A thought fluttered through her head. If Paul was hurt he couldn't go off to war. He'd have to stay in Cincinnati and ride trolleys, eat penny candy, and chase silly girls.

But what if he wasn't hurt? What if he was dead? Alice rocked her brother's body back and forth. She stared at his closed eyelids, willing them to open.

Suddenly, a blue eye popped open, stared up at her, and closed in a wink. A broad smile grew on Paul's face. Alice shoved her brother off her lap, furious all over again.

"Gotcha," Paul exclaimed and grabbed Alice's wrist before she could escape. "Now help me up. I don't know if I'm still in one piece."

Alice pulled Paul to his feet, relief overcoming her anger. He examined his bleeding elbow which stuck out of his torn shirt sleeve, then rubbed his head. He groaned. "I seem to be okay, but I have a feeling I'll have a terrific headache in an hour or so."

Alice smiled. "Serves you right." She got serious for a minute and looked into her brother's eyes. "You'd better write me!"

"How's this? I'll write you a special private letter all your own and send it along with the family's letter."

"Every time?"

"Every time."

"You'd better." Alice grabbed her brother in a bear hug.

# Chapter Three

Cool air blasted through the open trolley-car window and sent Alice's hair whipping around her face. Alex, sitting beside her, covered his laughing mouth with a hand.

"What's so funny?" Alice asked him.

"Your hair looks like a tornado!" Alex said, laughing openly now.

Alice gave Alex a friendly punch on the arm. "I'd close this silly window if it wasn't for that new flu epidemic rule."

"It's a good rule," Alex said loudly over the wind. "Dr. Evans came into the store yesterday. He told Mama fresh air may help stop the influenza."

"And staying out of crowded places," Alice added. "But almost nobody has influenza in Cincinnati. Father read in the paper last night there were only six cases out of the 400,000 people living here." Alice pulled her hair back with her hand to stop it flipping around her face. "Six people sick and now we have to put up with cold air and our hair flying all over."

Alice watched Ben sitting in front of her with Mama. He clasped his little hands over his hair as if he were trying to keep it attached to his head. She smiled. Mama chatted across the aisle with Mrs. Beck, Alex's mother, as Ellen held her hair out of her face with one hand while reading a book.

"My hair's fine," Alex said smoothing his wavy dark locks. Alice rumpled his hair and turned to watch the stores and houses pass by the open window.

The weather was nice for an early October Saturday, but the breeze sent a shiver down Alice's back. Her thoughts turned to her last ride in a trolley-car.

The trolley had taken the family to and from the train station to say good-bye to Paul. Paul had sat next to her just as Alex sat by her now. He had struggled to keep up his usual conversation and jokes, which had been fine with Alice. She had not felt like laughing.

At the train hugs and good-byes had seemed dreamlike, unreal.

As the train disappeared from sight, Alice strained for final glimpses of her brother. And then he was gone. Alice had pinched herself to awaken from the nightmare. Surely Paul would pop out of the train station laughing at her tears, calling, "Gotcha!" But Paul had not returned. And all that was left was a giant hole in Alice's heart.

That emptiness was still there as Alice rocked along in the windy trolley-car.

"You're awfully quiet," Alex said, readjusting his wire-rimmed glasses.

"Just thinking about Paul," Alice replied.

"Yeah, it's hard. I miss Father all the time."

"I don't know how you can stand it. Your father's been overseas so long."

"Over a year now. Sometimes I just lay on my bed and stare at his photograph—memorizing what he looks like."

They grew silent, in their own hurt-filled worlds. Alice pictured the formal black-and-white image of Alex's father. He was a grown-up version of Alex, same dark wavy hair, same glasses. She'd seen the picture countless times. Alice wondered if Paul would stand side-by-side with Mr. Beck, fighting the evil Huns. She prayed the war would be over before Alex too had to join them overseas.

Alice's thoughts turned to another photograph, the one of her family Mama had insisted on having taken before Paul left. In the black-and-white picture Paul stood next to Alice, face serious, but eyes twinkling. Alice's hair was neat and shining for the only time in memory; even her hair-bow was straight. Dressed in their best, the rest of the family stood tall and gazed solemnly into the camera.

She also knew what Alex meant when he talked about memorizing his father's image. So many times in the past couple weeks, Alice had taken that photograph off the mantle and studied the faces, especially Paul's. She had imagined being able to pull him out of that black-and-white world and into her own once more.

Alice shook off the sadness filling her heart. Today was a happy day. The two families were off to the zoo. "What are we doing? Paul and your father would want us to have fun! Remember our last zoo trip?"

"July." Alex smiled, the sparkle returning to his blue eyes. "Remember Paul at the reptile house?"

"Yes, he was chasing me around, like an alligator. I almost fell into the real alligator pit trying to get away from him." She laughed at the memory.

"Paul made faces at the monkeys and one threw food at him!"

"Yeah, and he threw it right back through the bars!"

The pair was still laughing at "Paul stories" as the families disembarked and headed for the zoo entrance.

Mama and Mrs. Beck each carried a wooden woven picnic basket. Ellen walked with her nose in her history book, seeming not to notice when her surroundings changed from houses and shops to lions and elephants. Alice couldn't understand her sister. Why did she have to make use of every second of her time? Why couldn't she just have fun like a normal person? Wasn't the family enough entertainment? Alice felt like throwing Ellen's book through the bars to a pacing, hungry-looking grizzly bear.

Instead she turned her attention to Ben and Alex who were studying the black bears. Alex was explaining to Ben what the bears ate and where they lived in the wild.

"They sure are messy," said Ben about the drooling creatures. "And they stink!" He pinched his nose, hopped from the little ledge he was standing on, and skipped to the mothers. Mama and Mrs. Beck looked content resting on a park bench, watching the bears from afar.

"I'm glad we could come today," Alex said, watching his mama. With Mr. Beck overseas, Mrs. Beck had been working constantly at their family grocery store. Alex helped after school and an elderly couple, the Wenners, and Mr. Price, a man in his twenties with a withered arm, worked too. But Mrs. Beck worked hardest of all. The Wenners and Mr. Price had insisted Mrs. Beck take the day off. They were running the store for her today.

The families walked toward the next set of cages—the monkeys. Ben dragged a stick across the brick walkway, the trunks of trees, the bars of cages. Ellen continued to read her book even as she walked along, pausing only to tell Ben to quit it. The mothers followed behind the group.

"I'm surprised the Wenners still work at their age," Alice said to Alex.

"The work's hard on them. You don't realize how heavy a bushel of apples or a sack of flour is until you try to lift one. I think they only stay on because they know Mama needs them.... But what she really needs is Father home."

For about the thousandth time since America had joined the Great War eighteen months ago, Alice was thankful her father worked for the post office. She used to hate his long hours, especially around the holidays. But he couldn't be drafted into the war because he was a necessary government employee. Each evening he walked in the front door, safe and sound.

But now she had Paul to worry about.

"Your father was drafted, but my foolish brother joined up on purpose! He doesn't think!"

"I've heard that said about someone else," Alex said.

"Fine, sometimes I don't think things through, but I wouldn't be stupid enough to join a war."

"I'd go," Alex said quietly.

"What?"

"I said I'd go. I wish my father was home and safe, but I'm proud of him. And I'd join up if I was old enough."

Alice threw her hands into the air, then thrust them onto her hips, disgusted.

"Boys! I'll never understand them! I thought you were different."

"Why? Because I like to read? Because I have a girl for a best friend?"

"No, because I thought all that reading would make you smarter. And being around me should too."

"I think it *is* smart to join up," Alex said defensively. "I don't want the Germans taking over our country."

"Me either. I'm glad the doughboys are protecting us. I'll spend all day knitting sweaters and dipping candles if they need us to. And you know how much I hate knitting, even more than history. I just don't want Paul, or you, or anyone I know to go overseas."

"That's selfish."

"I can't help how I feel. Instead, should I want people I cared about to go over there to be killed?"

"Of course not. Then I'd think you were crazy." Alex gave her a wry smile. "Like these monkeys." One monkey was hanging by one arm from the ceiling of the cage while another tugged on his dangling foot. A third paced, stopping every once in a while to tug on the bars, like he was trying to escape. Alex mimicked the monkeys and whooped.

Alice felt her frustration and anger drain out through her toes. She laughed.

"Let's not argue about this any more. Last time I talked about this Paul ended up falling out of a tree."

"He had help."

"Yeah, yeah." Alice gave Alex a playful shove and took off. "Race you to the reptile house."

The day went fast and Alice was surprised to find that for small patches of time she forgot Paul was gone. Maybe these blissful, forgetful blanks in time would grow bigger as the days went by. Maybe eventually she'd be able to think about Paul without imagining him lying on a battlefield, bleeding to death. Maybe.

The families made their way to the entrance of the zoo to go home. Now, Ellen carried her book at her side. As the day had progressed she had spent less and less time reading and more and more time watching the animals and talking with the adults and Ben. Mama and Mrs. Beck discussed a new chicken pie recipe Mrs. Beck had found in a magazine.

Ben spun in circles, twirling their empty picnic basket around his tiny body. Alex walked quietly beside Alice, a pleasant smile on his face.

Alice treasured this picture in her heart. Everything would be okay. Paul would come home safely and join them for another fun day at the zoo. The war would end and America would return to normal.

As they reached the entrance, the families found their way blocked by people clustered around the gate. An official typed sign posted on the gate read, *The Cincinnati Zoo will be closed until further notice due to the influenza epidemic. The United States Department of Health.*

# Chapter Four

"Alex! Alex! Did you hear? Alex!" Alice pounded on Alex's bedroom window again. The trellis she had climbed to reach his room wobbled with her wild movements, and she nearly slipped in her fancy Sunday shoes. "Alex, wake up!"

The window clattered open and Alice almost knocked on Alex's nose.

"I'm awake—now." He wedged the wooden brace under the window to hold it up, then rubbed a bleary blue eye. "Could you please tell me why I'm awake? It's not even a school day."

"You can catch up on your sleep anytime. School's closed!"

"Really?" He scratched his forehead with his finger, pretending to think. "Maybe that's because it's Sunday."

"No, school's closed because of the influenza epidemic. Maybe for a long time."

Alex sobered and stared at Alice in disbelief. "Are you sure?"

"Father read it in the paper last night. Schools are closed until further notice." She ticked off places on her fingers. "So are churches and theaters and moving picture houses and…"

"Stores? What about stores?" Alex's voice was sharp.

"Stores are still open."

Alex blew out the breath he'd been holding. "Thank goodness."

Alice mentally scolded herself. Here she was, so excited about school being closed, she hadn't even thought that Alex's family could lose their livelihood because of the epidemic. "I'm sorry, Alex. I didn't even think of the store."

"I understand. School being closed is a big deal." He paused, then continued. "I'll miss it."

"You're looney. I won't! No more history lessons to memorize and essays to write for Miss Lang."

"We'll still need to knit sweaters for the doughboys."

"You're right. And now we'll have more time for that. And more time for fun."

"I'll probably have less time."

"Why?"

"If the stores could close any day like other businesses, we'll probably have even more customers than usual. People may be lined up out the door to stock up on things. Mama will need me."

"They couldn't close the grocers. Where would people buy food?"

"I don't know…"

"Alice!" Alice looked down and found Ellen, scowling up at her, hands on hips in her blue satin dress. "There you are! I've been looking everywhere for you. We're ready for church."

"Church is closed, remember?"

"Of course I remember," Ellen said impatiently, "but Father wants to start our church service at home at the usual church time."

"I'm coming," Alice said. She turned back to Alex to finish their conversation and squished her face up in an exaggerated copy of Ellen's annoyed expression. Alex smirked, then quickly covered his mouth.

Ellen warned, "Mama'd skin you alive if she knew you were climbing trellises in your church clothes." Ellen stalked off toward home.

"Bye, Alex. See you this afternoon?"

"Meet you at your tree."

Alice quickly scampered down the trellis like a monkey at the zoo. She hopped down at the bottom and hurried after Ellen who was already striding into their own yard next door.

"Please don't tell! Please!" Alice begged.

Ellen kept walking.

Alice tried again. "I'll do your chores for you today!"

"There aren't very many chores. It's Sunday, remember."

"All right, I'll do them tomorrow."

Ellen paused on the porch steps. She turned to Alice. "All right. I'll just tell them I found you at the Becks' house."

"Thanks!" Alice gave Ellen a quick kiss on the cheek.

"But if they ask me what you were doing there, I'll have to tell them."

Alice rolled her eyes, then darted into the house.

Much to Alice's relief their parents did not ask what Alice had been doing. They were assembled in the parlor, with four dining room chairs arranged in two short rows like pews. Mama and Ben were sitting at Grandma's well-polished piano and Father stood beside the tall instrument. The girls moved to Mama's side and she played the first hymn. Everyone chimed in and "Amazing Grace" filled the house. The music was melodic and joyful, but Alice missed Grandma's elaborate playing and Paul's rich baritone. She even longed for Grandpa's tuneless gusto. At least she could listen to his rousing rendition of "K-K-K-Katy" or "Over There" on his next visit.

After several hymns the mini congregation sat in the chairs as Father, replacing Pastor Grady for the day, read from the Bible. Alice listened dutifully through the first few chapters, but eventually her thoughts drifted.

What should she do with all her new free time? She could sit in her maple tree—and do what? She could play in the creek, but she was getting a little old for that. Miss Lang would like her to work on memorizing history dates and writing. Yuck. She could finish the quilt she was making Grandpa Brockmann for Christmas. All those tiny stitches—maybe not.

She could write Paul. But she already did that most days.... Besides, she was angry at Paul. Paul's first letter home had arrived yesterday to the family's great relief. Alice had clung to every word Father read and pictured all that Paul wrote about. But she could barely sit still anticipating her own special letter from the other pea in her pod. Boy would Ellen and Ben be surprised. Probably jealous. But Father folded up the letter and slipped it back into the envelope without another word. Alice stared at him, mouth hanging open.

"What is it, Alice?" Father asked. "Trying to catch flies?"

She managed to close her mouth and say, "Nothing." She wasn't going to share her disappointment with the entire family. Maybe Paul had been too busy to write a second letter. Too busy for her? She'd let him know what she thought of that. And she had. A scalding letter to Paul lay on her writing table waiting to be mailed.

Lost in her thoughts she was surprised to look around the makeshift church and find everyone staring at her.

"Did the Bible reading make you mute?" Father asked her.

"No, sir," she said, confused.

"Then tell us the hymn you'd like to sing before it's Christmas."

By Sunday afternoon Alice had changed into her yellow cotton dress and was staring into her maple tree's reddening leaves. She lay across several branches, her arm swinging freely toward the ground. Ben's stick splashed in the creek below as he played with the crawdads. Ellen and Mama were inside knitting war sweaters and had asked Alice to join them. Alice couldn't bear to start a new war sweater so soon. She'd just been freed from school and the lumpy brown sweater waiting for her there, half-finished. She had volunteered to watch Ben outside while she waited for Alex.

Where was Alex? She checked their tree mail slot. Empty. She felt like she'd been waiting for hours. Actually she had only finished the dinner dishes about an hour ago, at 1:00, but Alex should have been here by now. They only had two people's worth of plates and silverware to wash up. As she waited, her mind flitted from thought to unrelated thought like a butterfly alighting on different flowers. Paul (the traitor), the war, chores, the flu epidemic, then Alex again.

What if Alex had gotten sick? Was that why he hadn't come? He was around many different people at the store. Had one of them been ill? No, that was crazy. No one they knew was actually sick with the influenza or "Spanish flu" as people were calling it. Alex had looked fine that very morning. He'd be along any minute. Or would he?

Worry filled her heart as Alice stared into the fiery branches.

Something slapped her hand. She rolled over to find Alex smiling up at her.

"Where have you been?" she asked, relieved and indignant.

"Helping Mama stock shelves."

"On a Sunday?"

"Mama didn't like to do it, but she was worried about the crowds come Monday."

"She must expect gobs of people if she's willing to work on Sunday."

"She's expecting a lot." His eyes grew troubled. "Please don't tell your parents she had to work on Sunday. She feels bad enough already."

"I won't. Come on up." Alex climbed into the tree and sat on his usual branch. Alice continued, "You had me scared to death."

"Why, I'm not very late."

"I know. But I guess that flu has me a little worried."

"That Spanish flu scares me, too. It's killed hundreds of people in Philadelphia and Boston." He paused and added quietly, "And in many army camps too."

"I know," Alice said softly. "I hope Paul's still all right, even if he is a louse." She told him about the letter that came and the letter that didn't.

When she finished Alex said, "I got a letter from Father yesterday, too. We were getting worried."

"How is he?" Alice asked.

"He'd be better if people weren't shooting at him and he could keep his feet dry." Alice grimaced as Alex told her about life in the trenches. This was Paul's future world.

Their talk circled through the war, family, the flu, and ended in silence. Alice lay staring at the leaves several moments, then sprang to a sitting position. "I don't want to think about the flu anymore. I'm sure we'll all be fine." Alice tried to believe her own words. "Let's have fun with our time off. Any ideas?"

"You're asking me?"

"Nothing good's come to mind."

The two sat silently in the tree for several minutes, thinking.

Alex said, "We could build a Ferris wheel or carousel with my erector set."

"Maybe some other day. I feel like being outside. It's a nice day."

Ben's sing-songy voice floated up to them. Alice thought he was telling the crawdads a story. Something about riding a bicycle to the grocery store…and going to Mrs. Schneider's, the neighbor lady's, to eat cookies. An idea popped into her head.

"Let's explore the neighborhood!" she exclaimed.

"What?"

"We'll just walk around here and see what other people are doing."

"But the flu!" protested Alex.

"Flu, schmu. If we see anyone with the flu we'll go the other way. And we can wear these." She pulled a handful of gauze and strings out of her pocket. Alex looked at her quizzically. "Masks! We'll be fine."

Mama, Ellen, and Alice had spent Saturday evening stitching

gauze masks. The paper had recommended wearing them to prevent the flu.

Alice tossed Alex a mask and tied one over her own mouth and nose.

She was poised to jump from the tree when Alex asked, "What about Ben? Aren't you supposed to watch him?"

Alice stopped. Ben. Ben had been getting in her way since he was born.

The night of Ben's birth filled her mind like it was yesterday: Father pacing in the front room, Mama crying out in their bedroom. It took so long that finally Alice, Ellen, and Paul were sent to the Becks' house to spend the night so they could get up for school the next day. Alice hadn't slept a wink worrying if Mama was all right. Alex, eight like her, had stayed up all night talking to her to help her feel better. That was the night they had become friends.

The next morning Mrs. Beck had greeted her with the news that she had a baby brother named Ben. And he'd been tagging along ever since.

"We'll have to take him with us," Alice decided. "If I send him inside, I'll have to go in too and knit. Yuck."

"Are you sure bringing Ben's a good idea?"

"He'll be fine." Pointing at her covered face, she said, "Masks, remember?" She leaped from the tree, landing on her feet.

As Alex climbed out of the branches Alice collected a protesting Ben.

"You made me lose him," he whined, pulling his arm away.

"Come on, Ben! You can watch crawdads any time. This will be fun…. You'll get to wear a neat mask."

Ben seemed to be considering her words. His head cocked to one side he eventually said, "I guess. Gimme my mask."

Alice tied a mask around Ben's head, careful not to catch his hair in the knot. All that was left of Ben's face were two nervous eyes.

# Chapter Five

The streets were quieter than usual, even for a Sunday afternoon. The porch swings and steps were empty. No kids had collected for a game of stick-ball. One lonely Model-T was pulled to the curb down the street. It was eerie.

"Where are the people?" Ben mumbled through his gauze mask.

"I don't know, Ben. Maybe they're all reading the paper or taking a Sunday afternoon nap."

They passed old Mrs. Schneider's house across the street from the Brockmann home. The curtains rustled, then Mrs. Schneider opened the front door and called, "What are you children doing out on the road? Is that you, Ben?"

"Yes, Mrs. Schneider," Ben answered.

"It's me, Alice, and Alex and Ben," Alice loudly explained. "We're going for a walk."

"You'd better get back inside, children. The influenza'll take you for sure."

Ben's frightened eyes stared into Alice's. She took his hand and shouted back to Mrs. Schneider. "We'll be fine. Just taking in some fresh air. Fresh air's good for keeping away the influenza. Have a nice day, Mrs. Schneider." Alice gave Ben's hand a tug and the three masked children headed down the deserted street.

Two tiny faces stared back at them out their next-door-neighbor's picture window. Alice waved at four-year-old Anna Longwell and her little brother Caleb. Two small hands shot up to wave back.

They passed Reverend Grady, their pastor, walking down the road. He tipped his hat to them and continued walking, holding a mask closer to his face.

Coming to the corner, Alice looked down the crossing street to see if anyone was about. A young lady stumbled slowly down the street. Alex said, "I wonder what's wrong with her."

The trio continued to watch the lady's slow progress toward them. "I'm scared," Ben said. He gripped Alice's hand tighter.

"It's all right, Ben." Was it?

"What if she has the flu?" Ben asked in a shaky voice.

"We don't know what's wrong with her, Ben. Besides, she's a block away from us. Just stay calm."

The lady coughed violently and fell to the ground. Ben jerked his hand from Alice's and flew toward home, faster than Alice had ever seen him move.

Alice turned from her fleeing brother to the sick lady. "We've got to help her."

"You said we'd turn around if we saw someone with the flu. We could catch it!"

"Maybe she doesn't have it. Anyway, I'm not letting a lady die in the street."

Alice took a few tentative steps toward the woman who was trying to stand. As she drew closer the woman's soft brown hair and blue eyes grew familiar. "Miss Lang?" How could her teacher be this sick and this far from home? She lived about six blocks away. Alice ran to her. "Miss Lang, it's me, Alice. Let me help you." She gently pulled the woman to her feet.

Miss Lang struggled. "No, Alice," she said in a weak, raspy voice. "I'm sick with the influenza. Get back."

"You need help, Miss Lang. Where are you going? You should be home in bed."

"Hospital," she gasped.

Alice thought quickly. The trolley stop was three blocks away.

"I'll help you to the trolley."

Miss Lang nodded, then left her head resting on her chest. Alice tugged a mask from her pocket, working to untangle the strings with one hand as she supported Miss Lang. Fumbling to tie the mask around Miss Lang's head, Alice nearly toppled over.

Alex walked quietly up to the struggling pair and gave Alice's arm a squeeze. He put Miss Lang's dangling arm over his back so that she was supported between himself and Alice. Once the mask was tied, the three took one step, then another, then another. The process was slow, but Alice thought they could do it.

Two blocks later, Alice wasn't so sure. Her back and shoulders ached and all three of them had tumbled to the brick street twice. Miss Lang's mask had grown alarmingly red each time she coughed.

With each step Alice prayed they'd have the strength to make it.

Finally, they reached the corner where a metal sign attached to a light pole read, Car Stop. Alice nearly fainted with relief. Seconds later the trolley rumbled to a stop in front of them. It was empty except for the conductor in his enclosed cubicle and the motorman. Alice climbed the first step, then dragged Miss Lang by her armpits while Alex helped her get her legs on board.

The conductor knocked on his glass partition and asked, "What's wrong with the lady?"

"She needs…to get…to the hospital," Alice grunted between tugs. They settled Miss Lang into the first seat.

"Does she have the influenza? I can't have her on here if she does."

"She'll die if she doesn't get to the hospital," Alice said forcefully.

"I'm sorry she's sick, but…"

"Please, sir. If you leave us here she'll die. You could have her to General Hospital in under ten minutes. Please."

The man considered the situation. "I don't wanna leave no woman to die, missy, but…" His voice trailed off and was lost beneath Miss Lang's violent coughing.

"Please."

"You haven't even paid to ride," the conductor complained.

Alice fished in her dress pockets. Nothing but tangled gauze and strings. Alex pulled three nickels from his pocket, showed them to the driver, and dropped them into the metal collection box.

"Fine, I'll take her, but I'm not picking up any more passengers with her in here." The trolley jerked forward and continued its route. Alice sat beside Miss Lang to hold her up as the trolley swayed. She seemed to grow weaker by the minute.

The trolley clanged as it arrived at the impressive, new General Hospital, touted as the best hospital in the world. Alex and Alice jumped up before the car had stopped rolling, yelled thank you to the driver, and got Miss Lang to her feet. Alex jumped down the steps and caught Miss Lang as she fell like a limp rag doll. Alice hurried down after her to help.

"Good luck," the conductor yelled through his glass wall. "You children sure have a lot of gumption. Hope you know what you're doing." The trolley clanged, then jolted forward once again, continuing on its way.

The three stumbled into the hospital. The main entrance was bustling with people. No wonder there was no one on the street or in the trolley-car. It looked as if everyone in Cincinnati must be here. People lay on stretchers along every wall of the fancy lobby. Nurses and doctors rushed here and there. An anguished cry rang out near Alice. She turned to find a nurse pulling a sheet over a young man's face while an equally young woman threw herself onto the man's body and sobbed. Cries of pain and grief from every corner of the cavernous room filled Alice's ears. The coughing and crying were deafening.

Alice, who had momentarily been frozen to the spot, took several steps into the nightmare. A nurse hurried by. "Excuse me," Alice called, politely. No response. Another nurse rushed past. "Excuse me," Alice said louder. This woman too went on. Finally, a third nurse walked by. "Please, help us," she practically screamed. "Our teacher needs a doctor."

The woman turned to Alice and said curtly, "So does everyone here. We're doing our best. Find an empty stretcher and we'll get to you when we can."

Alice and Alex searched the rows of white stretchers, looking for one without a writhing body on it, or a still one for that matter. "There's one," Alex shouted over the din. They half dragged, half carried Miss Lang to the empty stretcher. It was still warm from the last occupant. Alice shuddered. The last person to use this stretcher had probably died and been taken away. She yanked her mask off and vomited onto the floor.

As Alice wiped her mouth on her sleeve she looked around the room. Amid the chaos and pain no one even noticed a fourteen-year-old girl vomiting as she and a friend tried to lift their dying teacher onto a dead man's stretcher. Everyone in the room had a similar burden. She wanted to cry, but knew she couldn't.

Alice slipped her mask back on and helped Alex maneuver Miss Lang's body onto the stretcher. Once she was settled, Alice smoothed the woman's tousled brown hair back from her forehead. Miss Lang's pale blue eyes were filled with pain and thankfulness.

"Nooooo!" The long cry rang out behind Alice, startling her. At the next stretcher a young woman clutched a baby to her chest. The child was a lifeless doll. The distraught mother rocked the dead infant back and forth as a boy, about three years old, tossed and turned on a stretcher calling, "Mama, Mama." A third child, a little girl, sat at her feet, whimpering. The mother's eyes met Alice's. They were filled with unimaginable grief and weariness.

Feeling more helpless than before, Alice turned back to her teacher. She stroked Miss Lang's hair and looked into the sick woman's eyes. Miss Lang was trying to tell her something.

"What is it, Miss Lang?"

Alice and Alex each bent over the stretcher to try to hear.

"Go," said a quiet voice.

Alice argued, "But a doctor hasn't seen you yet."

"Go." The word was barely audible over the groans and sobs of the people surrounding them. Miss Lang coughed again, her mask turned redder.

Alice didn't want to leave Miss Lang alone, with doctors and nurses rushing past, no one helping her. But this room was filled with flu and she knew Miss Lang was trying to keep them safe. She and Alex had done all they could for her.

"All right. We'll leave if you want us to."

Miss Lang nodded. "Thank you," Alice thought she heard.

"Just get better, Miss Lang," Alex said.

Alice added, "Yes…we need you back at school…once it opens again…we need you to teach about the Battle of Gettysburg and how to diagram sentences properly."

Alice thought she detected a smile in Miss Lang's eyes. Then her eyes closed and she was still. Alarm shot through Alice's body. "Miss Lang? Miss Lang!" Alice shook the woman's body and her eyes opened halfway. She was still alive. Alice breathed a sigh of relief.

"Good-bye, Miss Lang," she said.

Alice turned to the mother next to them. Their eyes met over the sick teacher and dead infant.

Feeling overwhelmed, she took Alex's hand and they wove through the swarm of sick and dying people toward the door. At the end of the block, they stood side by side and breathed in the fresh, uninfected air.

They walked in silence toward home. No one would believe what she and Alex had been through together today. The eyes of Miss Lang and the grieving mother haunted Alice. Worry crept back into her mind. Had they done the right thing? They couldn't have left Miss Lang in the street. But now she'd exposed herself to the flu. And Alex too. According to the newspaper Father had read last night, the flu cases in Cincinnati had jumped to one thousand. What if one or both of them were the next people to lay on those stretchers, taking the warm place of someone who'd died moments ago, their families crying over their sick, pain-filled bodies?

She swallowed her fear and said, "I wouldn't believe it if I hadn't seen it with my own eyes."

"Me either. It was horrible. All that pain and dying. It's as bad as the war."

"It is a war. A war here at home."

Alex squeezed her hand and they hurried down tree-lined, quiet streets.

# Chapter Six

Alice waved good-bye to Alex, climbed the porch steps, removed her mask, and slipped in the front door. She had hoped to find the usual Sunday afternoon activities; Mama and Ellen still knitting war sweaters, Father reading the paper, and Ben playing with his tin soldiers or Lincoln Logs. Instead, panic filled the room.

Normally calm Ellen was pacing the room, muttering to herself. Father stared blankly over the newspaper, tapping his foot. Mama quickly rocked Ben in the rocking chair while Ben repeated over and over, "Alice, Alice, Alice."

All motion stopped as the family noticed her presence. Four pairs of eyes stared at her as if she were a ghost.

Ben jumped from Mama's arms and buried his tear-stained face in Alice's dirt- and blood-smeared yellow dress. "Alice, you're alive," came his muffled voice.

"Of course I'm alive, silly," Alice said, taking his head in her hands.

He looked into her face. "But that lady was sick." Ben hiccupped and began crying again.

"I know she was sick, Ben. But I had to help. Miss Lang needed me."

"Miss Lang?" Ellen asked, sinking onto the piano bench.

"Yes, I couldn't just leave her in the street to die. Alex and I took her to the hospital."

"You what?" Father bellowed.

Mama suddenly came to life. She snatched Ben from Alice's grimy dress and pushed him by the shoulder toward Ellen. She turned back to Alice, eyes ablaze. "Come. Now," she ordered.

Recognizing Mama's fury, Alice quickly followed her retreating back to the kitchen. Lips pursed, Mama dragged the largest kettle from the pantry, filled it with water, and clanked it onto the stove. She yanked Alice's filthy dress over her head, nearly taking Alice's ears and nose with it. Yellow material swirled around Alice's head, then jerked away. Pain shot through her scalp. Alice covered her mouth to stop a scream. Strands of brown hair clung to the dress buttons as Mama crammed it into the tepid pot of water. She grabbed the washing stick from the back of the stove, and poked furiously at the dress as if it were alive.

Goose bumps rose on Alice's bare arms. She rubbed them slowly, trying not to draw Mama's attention and wrath.

Mama turned from her dress soup. "Get to the tub!"

Alice hurried to the bathtub, turned on the water, then stood there dazed, watching the waterfall hit white porcelain. Why was Mama so angry? Mama woke Alice from her short trance by plugging the drain, then snatching each piece of clothing as Alice removed it.

Mama left quickly with the clothes and returned with a pig-bristle scrub brush, a bar of lye soap, and wrinkled clothes. "Get in."

Alice reached for the soap, but Mama said, "No, I'll do it."

Alice was mortified. "Mama! I can bathe myself."

"I'll do it." From her tone, Alice knew that was the end of the argument.

The bristles cut into her skin, forming red tracks across her arms and legs. Her skin tingled and stung. Alice bit her tongue to stop a yelp. The brush was taking off her skin along with the dirt and germs.

Mama dumped a bucket of water over Alice's head. She sputtered. All ten of Mama's fingernails raked Alice's scalp as she scrubbed at Alice's hair with the bar of soap. Another bucket of water cascaded over Alice's head. Then she felt the brush again on her sore neck and back.

Finally, Mama stood and grabbed a towel.

Alice jumped up to take the towel from Mama, nearly slipping in the shiny tub. Surely Mama would let her dry herself.

"Dry off and get dressed," Mama demanded, and was gone.

Alice worked quickly, afraid that at any moment Mama would hurry in and do it for her.

In the kitchen Alice found Mama stirring the pot of steaming clothes. "I cannot believe a daughter of mine has so little sense," she told the clothes. "Going to a hospital full of flu patients. Unbelievable."

"But Mama," Alice protested before she could stop herself.

Mama swung around. "Not a word, Alice Rebecca Brockmann." The silence in the room was punctuated only by the washing stick clunking against the pot. Alice froze, not sure what to do next.

Mama was shaking, Alice couldn't tell if it was from anger or crying. She turned to face Alice. "My sister Rebecca died of scarlet fever as a child." Her voice cracked. "That sickness nearly took us all."

Alice looked at the floor. "I know, Mama," she said softly. Alice knew about the aunt she was named for, knew that she had died of scarlet fever when she was eight years old.

"Papa brought the fever home when he was working on the railroad. Didn't mean to. He was just earning a living."

No wonder Mama was so angry. She thought Alice had accidentally brought the flu home to the family just as her father had done so many years ago. Alice looked into her mother's tear-filled eyes, then back at her bare feet.

"Now, I know you didn't mean to hurt anyone."

"No, ma'am," Alice said, tracing a crack in the floor with her big toe.

"But sickness is a dreadful thing. You must be careful."

"Yes, ma'am."

"Now, go back to your father."

Crossing the cold floor, Alice walked snail-like back to the parlor and Father. She was sorry she had scared Mama, but she was tired of being yelled at, talked to, and treated like a child. It would be terrible if she'd lost Paul, or Ellen, or Ben to a terrible disease. But Alice still couldn't have left Miss Lang in the street. That wouldn't have been right either. She didn't want to hear a second lecture from Father.

Reaching the parlor, Alice met the angry stare of her father over his newspaper. Here it came.

"Well, what do you have to say for yourself?"

Alice stared at her scratched red feet. She knew he was waiting for an apology.

"Well?" Impatience filled Father's voice.

Her words came in a loud rush. "I'm sorry I scared Ben and Mama and may have brought the influenza home. But I'm *not* sorry I helped Miss Lang. She needed me. And I'd do the same thing again."

Alice didn't give him time to react. She dashed past him and up the stairs, and threw herself across her quilt-covered bed.

Sobs shook her body. She waited for Father's angry footsteps on the stairs, belt in his hands. The Brockmann children were seldom whipped, but disrespect was not tolerated. She wondered how the strap would feel on her already scrubbed-raw skin.

# Chapter Seven

When Alice lifted her head from the quilt, the room was dim and filled with long shadows. She must have fallen asleep. The faint tingling of her scraped skin reminded her of her parents' anger and the future whipping. Father must be waiting until after supper. Alice crept to the door, opened it, and sat in the doorway. The bottom of the stairway glowed warmly with the downstairs gas lights. Father's voice drifted in bits and pieces up the stairs and through the floorboards.

He seemed to be reading something—not the newspaper—maybe a letter. He must be rereading Paul's letter. Despite her anger at Paul, Alice strained to hear. She missed him.

The muffled words came to an end. Chairs scraped on wooden floor and plates and glasses clattered together as they were removed from the dinner table. Footsteps grew louder and Alice ducked back into her room and quietly shut the door to await her punishment.

Someone walked up the stairs and knocked softly on Alice's door.

"Come in," Alice said as she sat on her bed in the dark.

The door opened slowly and Father came in carrying a tray. His belt snaked menacingly around his waist. "Brought you some dinner, Alice. Thought you'd be hungry after all your adventures."

"I am," Alice said, noticing her rumbling stomach for the first time.

"Let's get some light in here." Father set the tray on the girls' dresser, pulled a box of matches from his pocket, and lit the oil lamp next to the bed. "That's better."

Father sat on the bed and put the food between them. "You've had quite a day."

"Yes," Alice said. Her stomach churned, with hunger and nerves. She nibbled at a biscuit, but her flip-flopping stomach protested.

"Father?"

"Yes?"

"Can we just get my punishment over with? I can't take it

anymore." She slid to the floor and stood facing the bed, arms braced on the footboard, ready for her whipping.

Father remained seated on the bed and smiled. Alice looked at him quizzically. She knew some fathers took pleasure in whipping their children. A schoolmate, Naomi Trundle's father beat her hard and often, and Naomi'd secretly told her he laughed while doing it. Of course the rumor around school was that Naomi's father drank. But Father never touched alcohol, and had always looked sad before a whipping.

Father said, "I can't say what you did today was smart, but it was courageous."

Alice stared in confusion at her father, knuckles white from her firm grip on the footboard. Was he angry or not?

Father patted the bed. "Sit down. I'm not going to whip you."

Alice straightened and sat on the soft bed next to her father. "Really?"

"Really. It took a lot of courage to help Miss Lang. You put another's needs over your own."

"I thought everyone was angry with me."

"We were angry. And I think your mama and Ellen still have their feathers ruffled. You gave us quite a scare. We didn't know where you were. Ben flew through the door chattering about a sick lady. You did do a very foolish and dangerous thing."

"Foolish...but brave?"

"Yes." He continued, "We've taught you children to help people. And you're a spunky girl who saw a need and was brave enough to fill it. I can't very well punish you for helping a fellow human being."

Alice's heart rose and she smiled.

"However, I will punish you for taking Ben with you on your fiasco. That boy's only six years old and he scares easy. You should know better."

"Yes, Father."

"Your mama will expect some extra chores out of you this week. Maybe extra work will keep you out of trouble. And you will stay in your room this evening to think about the danger you put this family in, especially Ben and yourself."

"I will, Father." She gave him a hug, then grabbed a biscuit. More chores. It could be much, much worse. At least she wasn't forbidden from leaving the house or seeing Alex.

Father said, "People are getting sick all over town. More postal workers are sick every day. Mr. Jenkins worked with me yesterday and went home sick. He died last night."

"Oh, Father! I hope Miss Lang won't die."

"I hope so, too."

They sat a moment in silence. Father slipped a folded white piece of paper out of his pocket.

"The letter from Paul?"

"I thought you might like to hear it again. I reread it to the rest of the family at dinner. Thought it might brighten your evening, like it did your mama's."

Alice glanced at her letter to Paul on the desk, then said, "It will."

Father unfolded the letter and read.

*Columbus Barracks*
*Tuesday, October 1, 1918*

*Dear family,*

*I've just arrived at camp today. How's that for quick writing? I've received my uniform (I look pretty sharp in it) and the Y.M.C.A. has been kind enough to mail my regular clothes back to you. They've also given me this paper and even some stamps! I hope I'll have time to write. The guys who have been here awhile say it's a lot of work.*

*Mama, the food's edible so don't worry. Still, it doesn't match home cooking. I bunk with a lot of other guys and we sleep head to foot. They say that's because they're trying to stop us breathing on each other and spreading this disease called Spanish influenza. It's taken hold of quite a few men here. I think the work load's going to be worse than normal, what with doing drills and caring for the sick.*

*I hear there's church services here too. The Y conducts them on Sundays and I'll be sure to attend.*

*Time for bed. We have to rise at 5:30 a.m.—worse than for school Ellen, Ally, and Ben. Hope this finds you well.*

*Your son and brother,*
*Paul*


Father folded the letter carefully and slipped it back into his shirt pocket. Then he pulled out a second, identical looking sheet of paper. His eyes twinkled.
"What's that?" Alice asked. "Mail doesn't come on Sundays."
"You're right. But this comes special delivery to you."
Alice was confused.
Father went on. "There was another letter in Paul's envelope addressed to one Ally Brockmann."
"Why didn't you give it to me when it came?" Alice asked, reaching for the letter.
Father held it just out of her grasp. "Just one moment. I want you to know that it was not my idea to keep this letter from you."
"Paul!"
"Yes. He included a note asking me to wait a day or two to give you your letter. Something about getting you back for tossing him out of a maple tree."
"He *fell*. Ooooo. He makes me crazy."
Father shook his head. "Two peas in a pod."
He handed Alice the letter. 'For Ally' was scrawled in Paul's sloppy handwriting. She hugged the letter to her chest.
Father stood. "I'll leave you to your food, your letter, and your thinking. Don't forget about the thinking. Ben's young. We need to be able to trust him to your care."
"I know, Father, and I'm sorry."
Father stood. "Goodnight, dear."
"Goodnight."
The door closed softly behind him. Alice tore open her special letter.

*And In Flew Enza*

*Columbus Barracks*
*Tuesday, October 1, 1918*

Dear Ally,
 *Thought I didn't keep my promise, didn't you? Probably already wrote to tell me all about what a horrible brother I am.*

Alice gritted her teeth. He sure had fooled her.

 *Here's that special letter I promised you so you'd let me out of Cincinnati in one piece. There was a girl on the train who reminded me of you—brown hair, brown eyes and never stopped talking. I think she talked the man next to her's ear right off. I saw it laying on the seat when he got up—ha, ha. But it was kind of nice having her on the train since she reminded me of you. I miss your talking. The guys here talk mostly about the war, the influenza, and pretty girls they've met or hope to meet. Speaking of pretty girls, how's Vivien? You two would probably like each other if you tried. You both like to talk. Ha, ha.*

Alice scrunched up her face. Never.

 *I'll write again next letter, maybe. Ha ha. You make sure you write me back. Is everyone fine back home? I hear this influenza's not just in the army camps.*
   *Your promise-keeping big brother,*
   *Paul*

# Chapter Eight

Alice pulled her damp yellow dress from the wicker clothes basket and hung it on the line. Her hospital adventure ten days earlier had nearly ruined it, but with lots of scrubbing and several washings, she'd managed to get the dress clean. The scrubbing and prayers must have kept the flu away, also. No one in the family had fallen ill. Alex was fine, too. Alice had prayed every day for her family and Alex to remain healthy.

Grateful for not getting a worse punishment and for good health, Alice had worked hard at being responsible and doing her share or more than her share of the work. Mama volunteered at the Red Cross every day and Ellen usually went with her, so most of the chores and Ben-watching fell to Alice. Despite all the work, she had even started a new lumpy brown sweater for the doughboys.

She rolled the wooden cart holding the clothes basket across the grass to the next empty space on the clothes line and pulled one of Mama's everyday dresses from the damp pile.

The work wasn't too bad on the days Alex could join her. They'd lug water from the creek to pour on the pumpkins and squash in both families' war gardens, pull weeds, and read stories to Ben out of the large *Aesop's Fables* book with the golden lion on the cover. However, Alex spent most of his time at the store helping his mama, and by the time he got home in the evenings he was exhausted and it was too late for company.

Today, Alex was busy at the store as usual and Alice worked alone. Jamming two clothes pins onto Mama's dress to hold it in place, her mind wandered to better activities, better places. She was sick of chores, sick of knitting, sick of watching Ben, and sick of school being closed.

Alice had never thought she'd miss school—all that work. Since the war school had been even more work. Students were expected to knit sweaters and make candles for the troops on top of learning spelling, grammar, memory, math…. She missed walking to school in the crisp fall air, talking with her friends about schoolwork and boys, being somewhere other than home.

At least she knew that once school did resume, Miss Lang would be in the front of the room teaching. In shaky, but legible, handwriting, Miss Lang had thanked Alex and her for saving her life and reminded them to study while school was out. Alice knew they had done the right thing, helping Miss Lang. She couldn't wait to see her again at school, though Alice hadn't had much time to review arithmetic and history dates with all the chores to do.

Hanging Ben's knickers on the line, Alice dreamed of a world without war and influenza where she could ride trolley-cars, visit the zoo, have picnics in the park. Paul would be home playing blind-man's-bluff with them. No one would be attacking little villages in Europe and killing innocent people. Everyone would be healthy and happy.

A tap on her shoulder interrupted her thoughts. She turned.

"Alex!" Alice yelped in surprise.

"Mama said I could take the afternoon off. We weren't as busy as usual."

"I'm so glad to see you."

Alex grabbed Father's shirt from the basket and held it on the line for Alice to pin. "I'm glad not to be stocking shelves. I don't know how Mama did it with Father gone and me at school. She can't get enough help with the war on and the flu."

"Are the Wenners and Mr. Price well?"

"Mr. and Mrs. Wenner are fine, or at least as fine as they can be in their seventies. But Mr. Price's been home sick for a week. Didn't I tell you?"

"I don't think so."

"I think he's getting better, but it'll take awhile for him to get his strength back."

A child's crying rang through the calm Wednesday afternoon.

"Oh, no! Where's Ben?" Turning quickly to the stoop where Ben had been reading, Alice found it empty.

"He was on the stoop when I came," Alex reassured her. "He can't have gone far."

The back door slowly opened and Ben slipped out, carefully balancing his *McGuffey Reader* in one hand and a too-full glass of water in the other. He was concentrating, not crying.

The sobs continued, loud, but distant.

Alice said, "It sounds like it's coming from the Longwells' house."

Laundry forgotten, Alice ran toward the house next door calling, "Anna? Caleb?" Alex followed, also calling the names of the little children.

Four-year-old Anna Longwell sat on her porch step, hugging her two-year-old brother Caleb. Tears formed clean lines down the child's dirty cheeks as she squalled at the top of her lungs. Thumb in his mouth, Caleb snuffled and clung to his sister, looking bewildered.

Alice sat next to the children and put her arm around Anna's thin cold shoulders. The smells of sweat, urine, and feces invaded her nose. Both children obviously needed baths and the boy needed his diaper changed badly. Alice worked to ignore the stench as she calmed Anna. The girl's sobs quieted. Her breath came in sharp deep gasps, shaking her body.

Alex sat on the steps and held the boy's non-sucking hand. Caleb's stubby fingers curled around Alex's long ones.

When Anna calmed down, Alice asked, "What's the matter, Anna? Where's your mama?"

The children's unkempt appearance confused Alice. Anna was wearing a dirty, too-small, short-sleeved dress and Caleb's pants looked like they were on backwards. Usually the Longwell children were clean and happy, laughing as they ran through the backyard with their mother. Come to think of it, Alice hadn't seen them yesterday, but that was not too unusual. It was chilly out and the children probably played inside.

Through hiccups Anna said, "Mama's…sick."

"Does she have the flu?" Silly question. How would Anna know the flu from the sniffles?

The little girl shrugged and nodded.

Alice couldn't rely on the four-year-old's diagnosis. Mrs. Longwell needed help. They'd helped Miss Lang and nothing bad had happened, if you didn't count extra chores. Mama and Ellen were volunteering at the Red Cross and weren't home to say 'no.' She'd just have to help now, and face the consequences later.

"Alex, stay here with Anna and Caleb, while I check on their mama."

Alex leaned behind the children to whisper in Alice's ear. "Are you sure you should go in there? Maybe we could just call Dr. Evans."

She whispered back, "Remember the hospital? All the doctors are working overtime. It would take hours to get him here. I'll just be a minute."

Alice pulled a gauze mask from her dress pocket and tied it on. As she slipped through the front door, her eyes tried to focus in the gloomy hall. She shuffled her way toward the mother's bedroom.

Mrs. Longwell had been a widow for about six months, since her blond-haired, fun-loving husband, Len, had been killed in battle overseas. Although she remained cheerful and busy around her children, Mrs. Longwell had been devastated. Alice didn't think the children understood that their papa wasn't coming home. Since the awful telegram, Alice had spent many hours in the family's home caring for Anna and Caleb so Mrs. Longwell could catch up on her housework and have some time alone.

Now, the house was a shambles, as only two little children trying to care for themselves could make it. Entering the kitchen, Alice found bread crumbs, carrot tops, and a browning apple core littering the table. Anna had apparently tried to pour the milk from a pitcher. The result was a sour-smelling puddle dripping from the table onto the floor. Wooden blocks floated in the liquid like ships. A doll sat in a kitchen chair, mindlessly waiting to be served a meal. The ice box door was standing open, the food inside beginning to turn.

After shutting the icebox, Alice left the mess and continued to the bedroom at the back of the house. She heard groans coming from the twisted pile of sheets and quilts on the bed in a dim corner of the room. Alice tripped over Caleb's teddy bear as she entered.

"Mrs. Longwell?" Alice called softly as she reached the bed.

Her words were met with incoherent mumbles. Alice felt the woman's forehead. She was burning up with fever. Mrs. Longwell struggled for breath and her normally friendly blue eyes stared blankly at Alice, as if she didn't know her.

Alice worked at untangling the bed covers wrapped around the sick woman's body. The quilts stank with sweat and body odor, but Alice didn't have time to wash them right now. She pulled the covers neatly over Mrs. Longwell's writhing body and adjusted her pillow.

Entering the kitchen, Alice found a metal bucket turned on its side in the corner and a clean cloth in a drawer. She filled the bucket with water and returned to the bedroom. The water sloshed onto her feet as she stepped over the teddy bear.

Alice wiped Mrs. Longwell's face, neck and arms with the cool cloth. Then she laid the cloth over the woman's forehead and said, "We'll send for Dr. Evans, Mrs. Longwell. Alex and I are taking Anna and Caleb with us. You don't have to worry about them." Feverish eyes filled with pain stared back at Alice. The woman gasped for air then mumbled nonsense.

"You'll be all right, Mrs. Longwell," Alice tried to explain to the woman.

She stepped quickly through the dark house, opened the front door, and breathed in the sunny fresh air. Alex sat on the front porch, the children staring at him with big eyes. He was telling them a lion story.

Alice was out the door two seconds when Anna jumped up, threw her arms around Alice's waist and attacked her with questions. "How's Mama? Did you make her all better?"

Alice bent to the child. "Your mama's very sick, but we're going to fetch Dr. Evans to help her. You can come to my house and we'll fix you some food and get you cleaned up."

The child stared longingly at the door to her house, probably concerned about leaving her mama. Then her stomach seemed to get the better of her and she said, "Come on, Caleb. Alice and Alex have food!" Taking her little brother's hand, she helped him carefully down the steps, then began to run, dragging Caleb behind.

"How was she?" Alex asked quietly.

"I'm pretty sure it's the flu. She has a high fever. You'd better go call Dr. Evans. I'll change Caleb's diaper! Whew!"

Alice and Alex strode behind the children. Anna's matted hair bounced in gnarled strands off her back as she half skipped, half ran, nearly tugging her brother's grimy legs out from under him with her jolting movements. How would she care for these two little flu victims on top of her chores? What would Mama and Ellen say about her bringing them home?

# Chapter Nine

Ben still sat on the back stoop with his water and his book when the group returned from the Longwells' house. As the children approached him he wrinkled his nose and asked Alice, "What happened to them? They're smelly. And look at their clothes—they're all dirty!"

"Ben, watch your manners," Alice said. "Anna and Caleb have been taking care of themselves because their mama's sick. Run inside and start the bath water so I can get them cleaned up."

"Okay, but they'll make a ring in the bathtub. Mama will be angry when she gets home."

"Let me worry about that. You just go." Ben collected his glass and book and headed for the family bathroom.

Alice told the children, "You stay here and I'll bring you some food." Mama's kitchen was always tidy. Better to have the little ones eat outside until they were clean.

She ran inside, collected several apples, a loaf of fresh bread, and a knife from the kitchen, loaded it all on a plate, and returned to the hungry children.

Alex said, "I'll go to the store to call Doc Evans. Be right back." He took off running.

Alice wished for about the hundredth time that they had a telephone like the one at the Becks' store. It sure would be convenient, but Father felt they were more of a nuisance than a help. He said the Becks' store was near enough if they really needed a telephone. Who would she ring up besides Alex anyway? Rich, snooty Vivien Davenport? Never!

Vivien had bragged to Alice and Paul about her family's fancy new telephone and complained that the Brockmann house was "so behind the times." She saw Vivien in her mind, dressed in her fancy clothes, hanging on Paul's arm, simpering, "Oh, Paul. Do get rid of that silly little sister of yours. She's so wild—she's bound to dirty my new parasol." Ugh. What did Paul see in her?

At least Paul had stood up for Alice—sort of. "Oh, Vivien. Ally won't ruin your pretty things. Besides you'd be pretty as a picture in a ballroom gown or a dime store dress."

Vivien had smiled at Paul, then glared at Alice with her piercing blue eyes behind Paul's back.

Alice chopped savagely at the apple in her hand as she remembered.

"What's wrong, Alice?" Anna piped.

"Nothing a punch in the nose wouldn't cure."

Anna looked confused. Alice handed her the hacked-up apple slice. "Nothing's wrong, sweetie."

The children ate like starved animals, cramming the bread and apple slices into their mouths as fast as Alice could cut them. Crumbs and apple juice ran down their faces and arms and into the grass. Alice wondered how long it had been since they'd eaten a meal.

As soon as the fruit and bread had disappeared, Ben came to the door to announce that the bath water was warm and ready.

Alice stripped the children in the backyard, leaving the filthy clothes and diaper in the yard to wash later. Thinking of clothes, she glanced guiltily at the last few wet dresses and shirts wrinkling in the clothes basket. She'd probably have to re-wash them.

Alice hurried the naked children through the kitchen to the bathroom and plopped them both into the tub.

Scrubbing hard, Alice worked until the children's skin was warm, pink, and dirt free. She vigorously rubbed their hair with soap, worked on Anna's tangles, then dunked their heads under the water to rinse. Caleb came up sputtering and began to cry. Ben viewed the whole procedure from the bathroom door.

"Ben, watch them for a minute while I find some clothes for them to wear."

"What clothes?"

"Mama keeps our old clothes in the attic in the trunk. Be right back."

"My old clothes?" Ben asked protesting. "But they'll get them dirty!"

"You're too big for them anyway. I'll wash them later."

"Oh, all right." He turned to the children. "Caleb, sit down. You'll slip and hurt yourself," he instructed importantly.

*And In Flew Enza*

When Alice returned from the attic with a little red dress of hers for Anna and a diaper and outfit of Ben's for Caleb, she found a party in the bathroom. Anna and Caleb were laughing and splashing in the water. Alex had returned and sat on the toilet seat splashing too. Ben was in the far corner, attempting to stay dry, but smiling all the same.

Alice and Alex dressed the kids while Ben emptied the tub. Then the group settled in the living room to relax for a few minutes. Dr. Evan's wife had told Alex that the doctor'd been gone all day, but would stop in for messages in the evening. She'd send him right over when he came home.

Alice knew she should go over to the house and clean it up, but she was exhausted. As she watched Alex play Lincoln Logs with Ben, Anna, and Caleb, her heart felt warm and full. They were like a little family today; she and Alex were the mama and father, Ben, Anna, and Caleb the children. To the kids' delight, Alex balanced a Lincoln Log on his head. Alex turned and grinned at Alice. She returned the smile and joined them on the rug.

Steps sounded on the front porch and Mama and Ellen walked laughing and chatting through the front door. Their laughing eyes turned to questioning looks as they surveyed the little group in the living room.

"Hi, Mama! Hi, Ellen!" Ben said, jumping up and nearly knocking over the cabin they were constructing. He gave them each a hug.

"Hi everyone," Mama said. "We have some visitors this evening?" She raised her eyebrows quizzically at Alice. Ben returned to his cabin building with the children and Alex.

"Mrs. Longwell's sick, Mama," Alice said. "Anna and Caleb were taking care of themselves."

"Did you call Dr. Evans?"

Alex answered, "Mrs. Evans is sending him over sometime this evening."

"Is it the flu?" Ellen asked, her hand touching the mask she still wore from her trip home.

"I think so," Alice answered. "She has a fever and was having trouble breathing."

A scared look came over Anna's face as if she was remembering her mama's illness for the first time in hours. She began to cry. Alex took her into his lap.

"Alice, you didn't go in the house, did you?" Ellen asked.

"I had too. I had to see if Mrs. Longwell was all right."

"How could you?" she asked. She turned to Mama. "Mama! Now she's exposed us to the influenza all over again."

Ben stopped adding roof pieces and stood. He put his hand over his mouth and backed into Ellen's skirts.

"Now, Ellen," Mama said, removing her hat and coat, "I know we have to be as careful as possible about the influenza. But at the same time, we can't leave neighbors and their children without help because of our fears."

"But, Mama!" Ellen protested.

"Enough. I've been thinking about this for quite some time, since Alice helped Miss Lang to the hospital. Maybe she shouldn't have been gallivanting around town, but when she found Miss Lang so sick, she couldn't just leave her in the street. She was right to help. We're neighborly people. If we all came down with the influenza, God forbid, I would hope someone would come to help us."

Alice stared at Mama, mouth open in surprise. Now neither Mama nor Father was angry at her for helping Miss Lang. And Mama had corrected Ellen! That just didn't happen. The warmth in her heart grew.

"Mama?" she said. "Could we bring some soup over to Mrs. Longwell? And maybe clean up the house a little before the doctor comes? She'd be awfully ashamed if she knew the state it was in."

"Sure. Ellen, you get dinner on while Alice and I clean up the Longwells' house. Make soup and biscuits and we'll fetch some for Mildred if she's able to eat."

Alice asked, "Alex, do you want to clean or watch the children?"

"I think this log cabin needs a roof. What do you think, Anna?"

"Yep! A new roof! I'll help!"

Alice couldn't blame Alex for choosing play over work. She stooped to add a log to the cabin, accidentally brushing Alex's hand with hers. He smiled.

An hour later Alice and Mama returned, exhausted and hungry. They had cleaned up Anna and Caleb's kitchen mess, made Mrs. Longwell as comfortable as possible, and stayed until the doctor arrived. Mama had promised Dr. Evans to check on Mrs. Longwell every couple of hours until the fever broke.

The smells of potato soup and fresh baked biscuits filled the house as Alice and Mama came through the back door. Ellen had the table set and was sitting in the kitchen reading. Laughter rang out from the front room and Alice followed the happy sound.

Alex was crawling on all fours with Caleb on his back. Anna sat on Father's lap, laughing and clapping. Ben sat in a chair scooted as far to the wall of the room as possible, but sat on the very edge of it.

"Father, you're home! I bet you're starved."

"I'm mighty hungry." He bounced Anna on his knee. "I thought I'd come to the wrong house. I walked in the door and had three new children in the family."

Alex smiled and tipped Caleb off his back. "I'd better get home to Mama. She knows I'm here, but I'm sure she's waiting supper for me. G'night."

Alice followed Alex onto the front porch. The street glowed with pools of lamp light. The air was still and crisp.

"Bet you're more tired now than you would have been working at the store," Alice said.

"You're right," Alex said, massaging his shoulder.

Quiet enveloped the porch. Crickets chirped. Muffled laughter escaped the house. Alice felt peaceful and happy, and yet a little uneasy. She had never felt uncomfortable around Alex, but something new, something unspoken, now hung between them. She looked into Alex's deep blue eyes behind his glasses. He gazed back. Both quickly looked away.

"Well...see ya," Alex stammered.

"Okay," Alice replied, relieved to have the awkwardness dispelled by words. "See you tomorrow?"

"Maybe. It depends how busy we are. I'll try to come over." Alex slowly backed toward the porch steps, nearly toppling down them. He caught himself in time and climbed down. Halfway through the yard he turned to wave. Alice waved back as his form melted into the shadows. She leaned against the front door, her heart pounding.

# Chapter Ten

Alice stirred a frying pan of eggs as she listened to Mama's instructions. Mama had her hat on her head, a basket of supplies on her arm, and her mask in her hand, ready for a day caring for Mildred Longwell. Ellen was placing the warmed biscuits from last night into a basket. Father sat at the round kitchen table, dressed in his usual, a brown suit and white shirt. He juggled Ben on his lap and last night's newspaper in his right hand. He was in danger of dousing the lot with the cup of coffee inches from his right arm. Mama slid the coffee out of harm's way and continued speaking.

"Alice, I'm serious about you and the children wearing your masks at all times. I admire you for taking care of Anna and Caleb, but you must watch out for your safety also."

"I will, Mama," Alice said. She grabbed a pot holder, lifted the heavy skillet, and scooped piping hot, yellow mounds of eggs onto each plate on the table.

Mama continued, "Ellen, you take care of the house and chores. And wear your mask. Ben, you too."

You don't need to tell Ellen to wear her mask twice, Alice thought, watching her sister place the basket of biscuits on the table, only her blue eyes showing over her gauze mask. How did she plan to eat breakfast? Ben's eyes looked worried as he dug in his pocket for his mask and struggled to put it on.

Father took the little mask and laid it on the table. "After breakfast will be just fine, Ben." He stroked his tidy brown hair.

As Alice and Ellen joined Father and Ben at the table, Mama crossed the room and put a hand on Father's shoulder. "I'm sorry I can't call on Grandpa today. I hope he'll be all right until next week." Mama usually visited Grandpa downtown each Thursday to tidy his apartment and bring him some homemade cooking.

"He'll be fine, dear," Father replied, patting his wife's hand. "I'll check in on him after work and let him know you'll see him next Thursday."

"I put a couple extra biscuits in your lunch pail for him. I just know he isn't eating."

"Grandpa can't pass up your biscuits," Alice said, grabbing one out of the basket on the table.

"He's a grown man, Grace. He can take care of his needs for one week while you care for someone truly in need."

"I just worry. You know how stubborn he is—refusing to ride the trolley-cars except to come here. Ridiculous. People have been riding trolley-cars for years, but not George Brockmann. He only buys meat at Murphy's Butcher Shop, and bread at Gressler's Bakery." She ticked the shops off on her fingers.

"Don't forget sweets at The Corner Confectioner," Alice added.

"Rock candy! Mmmm!" said Ben.

"Peppermint sticks!" Alice added. "Grandpa's candy shop makes the best!"

"He'd do well to stay away from that place, Alice." Mama turned back to Father. "What if Murphy's or Gressler's closes because of the flu? He'll starve."

"You have enough to worry about without concerning yourself over my father and his stubborn ways. He'll be fine."

"If you say so, dear." She kissed him on the cheek, then continued around the table kissing each forehead. She set her basket down to don her mask, collected the basket again, and headed for the back door.

Muffled crying came from the front bedroom.

"Caleb!" Alice jumped up and started for the front of the house.

"Alice! Your mask!" Mama protested.

Alice fished the bothersome piece of cloth out of her large dress pocket, struggled with the ties, and hurried to the sobbing toddler.

The children were in a makeshift bed at the foot of her parents' bed. Caleb huddled in the 'v' made by Anna's sprawled skinny legs, his sister's arms wrapped around his little body. They sat in a tangle of quilts, Anna's nightgown slipping off one shoulder. Both children's skin looked pale, and they had dark circles under their eyes.

Alice hoisted Caleb out of the jumble of fabric and legs. He squirmed away, wrapping his arms around Anna's neck. "Mama," he cried.

"Where's Mama?" Anna asked in a tiny voice.

"She's sick, remember?" Alice said softly. "My mama's gone to your house to take care of her."

"Can we go see her?" Anna asked.

"Not until she feels better, Anna. I'll take care of you today. We can play together. Let's go have breakfast. I made eggs."

Alice reached for Caleb again. The boy looked at his sister who nodded and let go of him. Alice put Caleb on her hip and pulled Anna to her feet. "But first, it seems that someone needs a clean diaper. Is it you, Anna?" Alice asked, teasing.

Anna put her hands on her hips. "I'm a big girl," she declared. "Only Caleb wears diapers."

"You're right. Well, I think I'll need a big girl's help to keep Caleb still. Will you help me?"

"Sure. I help Mama with Caleb all the time."

After the diaper change, Alice dressed the children, then shooed them toward the kitchen. On her way out the door, she grabbed the two little masks on Mama's hope chest.

When they reached the kitchen, Father had left for work. Ben sat, mask on, practicing his writing on the edge of the newspaper with a pencil. Ellen was clearing the table of several empty plates. Alice pulled out a chair for Anna and settled Caleb on her own lap.

Ellen said, "Alice! Their masks aren't on!"

"They can't eat with them on, Ellen. I have them right here for when they're finished."

Ellen touched her mask, then opened the oven to pull out three plates of eggs and biscuits which she had kept warming for them. She scooted Ben out of the room and told him to brush his teeth and comb his hair. From the looks of it, Ben must have combed his hair several times today already. "And be sure to put on your mask!" Ellen called at Ben's retreating form.

The morning was filled with changing diapers, braiding hair, playing with dolls and blocks, and a short nap. Alice could have used Alex's help, but he was at the store, probably lifting heavy sacks of flour into place and straightening and filling the dry goods bins. After lunch, Alice promised, they would play in the backyard. The morning air had been crisp, but the afternoon was warming up nicely.

Alice hoped she and Ben could find enough to do to entertain the two children. She wanted to keep their minds occupied with fun and play. Looking into those tear-filled, round eyes full of sadness, fears, and questions broke Alice's heart. She didn't know how to answer their questions about the only parent they had left. Mildred Longwell was extremely ill and Alice couldn't lie to the children by promising them she'd be fine.

The foursome examined rocks in the creek, searched for crawdads, and jumped from stone to stone. One misstep by Caleb resulted in tears and the need for a dry outfit. Gathering up the wet boy and his indignant sister who wanted to remain in the creek, Alice trudged back to the house. Ben refused to help with what seemed to Alice like the tenth change that day. He had his eye on a big crawdad and he didn't want to lose it.

Alice found a dry outfit and diaper in the small pile of clothes she and Mama had brought back from the Longwell house last night. While she changed Caleb, Anna entertained herself by jumping on Mama and Father's bed.

"Anna, stop please," Alice said. Her words were jumbled by the diaper pins in her mouth, but she knew Anna understood. Still, Anna jumped, higher and higher. The bed springs squeaked in protest.

"Anna! Stop!" Alice said in a firmer voice as she struggled with Caleb who was squirming out of his diaper and trying to stand up.

"Caleb, stay here," Alice practically yelled in frustration. "Anna, stop this instance. You'll hurt your…"

Too late. Anna's foot slipped as she landed, and she tumbled onto the floor. Abandoning the half-naked Caleb, Alice rushed to Anna, who lay crumpled between the bed and Mama's wooden hope chest.

"Oh no! Are you all right?"

Alice's question was answered by the four-year-old's wails. Alice scooped up Anna and rocked her in her arms.

"There, there," Alice cooed. "You'll be fine. You just had a scare." She smoothed the little girl's braids and looked over to Caleb. He stood, diaper hanging from one hip, a puddle between his legs on the wooden floor. Alice groaned. How had her mother ever done it with four of them? She was about to go crazy with two.

Eventually, with the mess cleaned up, Caleb dressed, and Anna calm, they headed back outside to play. To Alice's great relief, Alex strode into the yard.

"Got the afternoon off. How's it going?" He smiled and looked at Alice from head to toe. She must look a wreck. She unconsciously smoothed her hair with her free hand, then readjusted Caleb on her hip.

"I sure am glad to see you." She handed Caleb to Alex, rubbed her tired arm, and smoothed her dress. "I'm exhausted."

"How about a game of chase, Anna?" He plopped Caleb onto the grass and ran after Anna. Anna squealed as Alex growled and took a swipe at one flying braid. Alice squatted to Caleb's level and duck-walked toward him. He toddled away from her, giggling.

The chase continued around the maple tree, through the garden rows and drying sheets on the clothesline, into the creek and out of the creek, disturbing Ben's crawdad search. Hands on hips, Ben announced, "I'm leaving. No crawdad would stick around with all this racket." He stomped across the grass headed toward the house, barely noticed by the chasing gang.

Jogging around the house after Anna, Alice noticed she had lost her mask somewhere. She thought it may have fallen off as she darted after Anna amongst the corn rows. She'd find it later.

Eventually the tired group collapsed in a giggling, rolling tickle fight in the front lawn. Alex's mask sucked in and out with each gulp of air. He slipped the mask off his mouth and onto his forehead.

"You look silly!" Anna said, pointing.

"Really?" Alex asked. He grabbed Anna and tickled her mercilessly. "I look silly?"

Alice flipped around to tickle Caleb's exposed stomach. Then she shrieked herself as Anna got an arm free from Alex and tickled Alice under her arm. Alex released his captive and helped Anna by pinning down Alice's arms and tickling her himself.

"Stop!" Alice gasped between giggles. Out of the corner of her eye she spied Caleb toddling toward the porch. "Caleb's getting away! Go get him! He needs a good tickling!"

Anna tore off to recapture her escaping brother. Alice got one arm free and managed to tickle Alex's neck and ears before he pinned her to the grass with both arms. Alice squirmed, then stopped. Alex's eyes were staring into hers, full of something. Confusion? Fear? Happiness? Alice couldn't tell. Her heart fluttered.

Suddenly, more than anything in the world, she wanted him to kiss her. He tilted his face toward hers. She closed her eyes.

# Chapter Eleven

Barely breathing, her eyes closed, Alice waited in the grass. She wanted Alex's kiss with all her heart. Screams and laughter invaded her private thoughts. Alex collapsed hard on her, jolting Alice's eyes open, as Anna and Caleb jumped on top of him. He rolled off her and crawled after the children, growling like a bear.

He seemed to have instantly forgotten the moment. Had she made it up in her head? Had he been planning to kiss her or not? Alice stood and brushed the grass off her dress, tired of the children's games. Heading toward the side yard, she left Alex with Anna hanging on his back, arms around his neck. They chased Caleb.

"I lost my mask," she called softly. Her voice shook a little. "Be right back."

She had to get away and think and looking for her mask was as good an excuse as any. Mama'd be furious if she came home to find her without it. But at the moment she didn't really care about Mama's mask rule. She wanted the stolen moment with Alex back. She wanted to know what he was thinking, feeling. They had always been able to talk about anything together. But she couldn't talk about this. What if he laughed? He probably wouldn't, Alex wasn't mean like that. But what if she was just a friend to him? A best friend, but only a friend? She didn't think she could bear that.

Arriving at the garden, Alice searched the rows, finally finding the wayward piece of gauze dangling from a rustling corn stalk. She yanked it off a large, pointy leaf. Plopping down next to a large orange pumpkin, she draped her arm around its ridged middle and rested her cheek on its smooth, cool skin.

There was nothing to do but go on. The moment was past. Maybe another chance would come along, if Alex felt the way she did. She'd have to wait and see. For now, she'd have to be happy with their friendship. She thumped the pumpkin, stood, and walked resolutely out of the corn.

Automatically, Alice went to the sheets billowing on the

clothesline to test them for dampness. Finding them dry, she mindlessly folded them neatly and piled them in the waiting wicker clothes basket Ellen had left. Feeling calmer, Alice tied on her mask and strode toward the front of the house.

She found Alex sitting on the porch steps, Anna and Caleb on each side of him. Ben was sitting on the far corner of the porch swing with his legs drawn up to his chest and his mask almost covering his eyes. Ellen's masked face stared through the big picture window in the front room. All were watching something across the street.

Alice turned to see a simple, long pine box carried out of the Schneiders' house by four men clothed in black. One of the men was Pastor Grady. And there was Mr. Schneider, eyes downcast, carrying the opposite corner of the box. Alice recognized the other two men as the Schneiders' grown sons, William and Jeremiah, who had families of their own across town.

But where was Mrs. Schneider? Someone in their family must have died and Mrs. Schneider would be heartbroken. She was always talking about her sons, their wives, and her grandchildren as she passed out cookies and chatted with the neighborhood children.

Alice recalled her most recent conversation with Mrs. Schneider. Both had been sweeping leaves off their porches and walks, fighting the swirling wind which insisted on carrying the leaves back to their original positions.

"Sweeping leaves in a breeze is like filling a bucket with a hole in it. You never finish," Mrs. Schneider had called through her mask, from her walk.

"I'm about ready to let the wind have the silly leaves," Alice had answered. "Maybe it'll blow them clean away."

"And just blow others right on in. It's a challenge, that's for sure, but I can't abide by a messy porch."

"At least I have Ben out of my way for awhile. He stayed inside. The wind messes his hair and flips his book pages."

"Now that boy's a mother's dream. Neat as a pin."

"I guess so, but Mama doesn't have to mind him all day. That's my job."

"A good job for a young lady like yourself. Get you ready for motherin'. My Jeremiah's wife's expecting their fifth any day!"

"That's wonderful, Mrs. Schneider. Are you hoping for a

grandson or granddaughter?"

"A little girl would be nice. Only have two granddaughters out of the eight grandchildren."

"Then I'll hope for a granddaughter for you, Mrs. Schneider."

"Thank you, dear." Mrs. Schneider had waved good-bye and shuffled inside, an unruly leaf landing on her porch before the door even closed behind her.

Alice watched for Mrs. Schneider's slumped form to slip out the front door behind the coffin, and wondered if at least she had a baby granddaughter to brighten this sad day. But no one else came.

Suddenly Alice knew that Mrs. Schneider was the family member who had died. She was in the coffin. She'd never know her grandchild, boy or girl. A lump grew in Alice's throat and tears filled her eyes. She leaned against the porch railing.

A sudden gust of wind whipped stray leaves onto Mrs. Schneider's tidy porch. It twisted gray paper streamers flowing from the Schneiders' doorway. Alice's fears were confirmed. With all the sickness recently, people had begun hanging streamers to indicate a death in the family—gray for the elderly, black for middle-aged, and white for children. The only elderly people in the Schneider family were Mr. and Mrs. Schneider.

The tiny procession carried the coffin to the waiting hearse. The chestnut horse at the front stamped and whinnied as Mrs. Schneider's casket was slipped into the fancy glass-sided wagon. As the hearse driver called for the horse to "git" the tiny procession followed.

All along the street neighbors stood in doorways and peered through windows. Mrs. Schneider would be missed. Normally a church full of family and friends would have said their proper good-byes to Mrs. Schneider. But Mrs. Schneider must have died of the Spanish flu.

To stop the spread of the flu, strict funeral rules had been made for flu victims. Only immediate family members were allowed. And the funeral must be held at home instead of in the church. The tiny group of mourners followed the hearse from the Schneiders' home to the nearby cemetery as the rest of the grievers watched from their homes, masks shrouding their sad faces.

At least Mrs. Schneider had a casket and a hearse, Alice tried to comfort herself. In other cities the epidemic had gotten so bad that caskets full of bodies lined the streets, waiting to be buried. People were stealing coffins for their dead and dying loved ones. The wooden boxes and graves could not be made fast enough. Alice shuddered to think that things could get that bad here, in Cincinnati.

As the funeral procession turned the corner toward the cemetery and crept out of sight, Alice slumped to the bottom step and put her head in her lap. The air was suddenly calm. Several birds chirped and soft sniffles came from the porch swing. How had this happened? Mrs. Schneider had been so careful about the flu. She always wore her mask and told everyone she met to wear one. And she had been so healthy only a few days ago.

A light tap on her shoulder made Alice look up. Anna's frightened eyes searched her own and the child crawled into her lap, throwing her arms around Alice's neck. "I want Mama," she cried weakly.

"I know you do, Anna, but your mama's sick."

"Will Mama get put in a box? Will she go away in a carriage?"

Alex must have explained the funeral to the children while she was in the back yard. Alice didn't know how to answer the questions. For all she knew, Anna and Caleb were orphans this minute. After all, Mrs. Schneider had been fine one day, gone the next.

After a pause Alice answered, "I hope your mama will be just fine, Anna."

She squeezed the child tightly to herself. Anna felt strangely hot for the cool October day. Alice stood, set Anna on the step, and removed the little girl's mask. No, Alice's heart screamed. Not Anna, too.

Alice had learned enough about flu symptoms to know that fever and the bluish tinge she saw on Anna's skin were signs. Inside she was panicking, but outside she knew she had to be calm for Anna. She replaced Anna's mask and picked her up in her arms.

"I think it's time for you to visit your mama right now," she told Anna in a pleasant tone. Her voice was calm, but her look to Alex was full of dread. "Alex, will you watch Caleb and Ben?" she managed to ask in a normal voice.

"Mama!" Caleb cried. He pulled away from Alex and toddled toward home.

Alex followed after Caleb and swung him over his shoulder.

"Hold on there, kiddo. Just Anna right now." Caleb squirmed and kicked.

Alice raced to the Longwells' front porch in seconds, Anna jostling in her arms. Careful of her bundle who was now strangely still, Alice climbed the Longwells' steps and fumbled for the door handle.

"Mama? Mama?" Alice called into the dark, quiet house.

Mama bustled out of the back bedroom.

"Mama, it's Anna. She was playing a little while ago. Then she crawled in my lap and I felt she had a fever. Look, her skin's blue."

Face drawn, Mama felt the child's hot, bluish cheeks and shook her head. Alice asked, "Should I lay her in her little bed in Mrs. Longwell's room?"

"Mama," Anna murmured.

"Might as well. It may comfort both of them." Alice hurried with her limp bundle past her exhausted mother. Pulling back the covers with one hand, she lay Anna in the trundle bed next to Mrs. Longwell's big bed. The children had slept in their mother's room ever since their father's death.

"Alice, I'll take care of Anna now. You go back home," Mama said quietly.

"Mama, Anna needs me," Alice said softly. Mrs. Longwell groaned under her pile of quilts and Mama rushed to her side.

Fear and pain filled Mrs. Longwell's voice. "Anna?"

"We're taking care of her," Mama comforted softly.

Alice slipped off Anna's dress and pulled a ruffled nightgown over the child's blue body. How quickly Anna's breathing had become raspy and shallow. Alice gathered another quilt from a cedar chest and a cool damp cloth for Anna's head. As she lay the cloth on Anna's burning forehead, Alice felt helpless. What good was an extra quilt and a wet cloth against a killer like the influenza?

She slipped to the floor next to the tiny bed and lay her head on Anna's still body. As tears flowed from her eyes, Alice stroked Anna's warm head. "Will Mama get put in a box?" Anna had innocently asked so recently. Now Alice wondered, would Anna get put in a box? Would they all get put in boxes? Would there even be enough boxes to go around?

# Chapter Twelve

Alice leaned her head against a rough branch in her maple tree. A scarlet leaf floated gently onto her still hands which clasped an unread letter from Paul. Mama had sent her home from the Brockmann's to rest, but as her body relaxed in her tree, her mind raced.

Anna had been a playful little girl yesterday and was now fighting for her life. Catching only moments of fitful sleep, Alice had watched over Anna all evening, through the endless night, into morning. After twisting and turning with fever for hours, Anna would suddenly grow still, panicking Alice.

Anna was alive, but for how long? Mrs. Longwell seemed to be doing slightly better, but would she get worse again? And who would get sick next? Mama, Father, Ellen, Ben, Alex? Would this letter from Paul reassure her that at least he was fine, or would it too be filled with sickness and death? What if Paul had fallen ill after writing the letter and was coming home to them in a coffin as she read it?

She tore open the letter. Maybe Paul had some good news on this cloudy, cheerless day.

*Columbus Barracks*
*October 11, 1918*

*Dear Ally,*
*Sorry I haven't written every day. I'm writing you an extra long letter now to make up for it. Things are busier here than I ever thought they could be. They work us morning till night. I know, you're probably saying—good, you deserve it.*

## And In Flew Enza

Alice smiled as she brushed another fallen leaf off her lap. She had been thinking just that. Paul knew her well.

> *Boy, am I sore from all the drills and parading around in our gear. When we aren't training we're taking our shift in the hospital ward. I've never seen such sick folk in all my days. And they go so fast. A bunk mate of mine, Charles, collapsed right in front of me in our parade line. We were marching in uniform in full gear for the officers. When I went to the hospital ward for my shift that afternoon, he was gone. Dead. I sat behind the bunk house and cried (our secret, please). How can the influenza be so deadly?*

This horrible disease was everywhere. No one was safe. She closed her eyes and said a quick prayer for Paul before continuing.

> *Please, don't tell Father and Mama about all the sickness here. I don't want them to worry. I don't want you to worry either, but I have to talk to someone or I'll bust. I'm strong as an ox and will be fine. I'll be home in plenty of time to embarrass you in front of visiting gentlemen callers. Or am I a little late? Has Alex already come calling? If he hasn't yet, he will, you mark my words.*

Alice blushed, hoping Paul was correct.

> *Speaking of "friends," I've written several letters to Vivien, but have not heard back recently. I know you don't like her, but I happen to enjoy her company, even if she does sometimes talk a bit much, like someone else I know.*

Ooooh! How dare he compare her to that tart again. She pounded her fist into the skirt of her dress.

> *Could you check on her for me? I haven't heard from her recently. Let me know how she is and give her my address again in case she's lost it. Thanks, Ally.*
> *Keep writing, please. I love to hear from you. You have no idea how welcome a letter from home is in this place. Mail-call is the best part of the day.*
> *Your big brother,*<br>*Paul*

Alice hugged the letter to her chest, then read it twice more. Pride filled her. She was the one person Paul could confide in, about the sickness in the camp, about crying over his friend. And he trusted her to talk to Vivien for him, not that she wanted to talk to that nasty weasel disguised as a beauty queen. In Alice's mind Vivien twisted a perfect strand of hair around a slender finger while hanging on Paul's arm and his every word. Alice rolled her eyes. Still, Paul cared about her and he trusted Alice to check on her. She'd do it this afternoon.

Guilt flooded into her heart, sweeping the pride out. Paul had told her everything that was going on at the camp, trusted her with things he had told no one else. Alice herself had not been so truthful in her letters to Paul. She had not lied to him exactly. She just hadn't mentioned much about the influenza epidemic. She hadn't wanted him to worry about the family. She had filled her letters with rambling stories about Alex and Ben and reported that Ellen was bossier than ever. Taking Miss Lang to the hospital had been hard to write about without mentioning the flu, but Alice had managed it.

Now she wished she had told Paul everything. If she had been away from home, she would have wanted to know the truth. She'd correct her mistake with her next letter.

Alice stretched and yawned, her muscles stiff from sitting up with Anna all night. Perching in her tree's branches didn't help matters. Despite her exhaustion, Alice knew sleep would not come. She'd walk to Vivien's for Paul; maybe the trip would make her sleepy. Grabbing a branch she swung out of the tree—and smacked hard into Alex.

Startled, Alice screamed and let go of the branch, landing on top of Alex who had been knocked to the ground.

Alex straightened his glasses and leaned up on his elbows. "Nice welcome, Alice. I'm glad to see you too." He smiled and rubbed his head. "It's dangerous to be around you and this tree."

Alice rolled off Alex and tried to regain her composure and her breath. She smoothed her hair with one hand while tucking her dress around her knees. "Sorry," she said softly. Sorry? Why did she apologize to Alex? She should have given him a friendly push and told him not to sneak up on people like that. What was wrong with her?

Alex gave her a quizzical look. "No problem," he said, sounding confused.

Alice's brain felt muddy. Had she hit Alex so hard she injured her head? She felt her skull and shook her head back and forth. It felt fine. She had to pull herself together.

"That's what you get for sneaking up on me," she said, her voice a little forced and unsure.

Alex's smile returned. "That's more like it. I was beginning to think something was wrong with you." He stood and pulled Alice to her feet with one arm. "How is Anna?"

"She was sleeping when I left her. I should go check on her again."

"Is Caleb still okay?"

"Ellen's watching him, though she's not happy about it. She's wearing two masks if you can believe it."

"How's Mrs. Longwell?"

"Some better. I hope *my* mama can hold out. She's exhausted, but she refuses to leave. Tonight I'm going to insist Mama go home to rest. I'll watch Anna and Mrs. Longwell. Mama made me come home and get some rest, but I can't sleep."

"Of course you couldn't sleep. You were sitting in a tree—not the most comfortable bed."

"I don't think I'd do much better in my bed. So I'm going to walk over to Vivien Davenport's house."

"Are you kidding? I thought you loathed her!"

"I know. And her mother's twice as bad—always sticking her nose up like we're not rich enough to walk down her block. But Paul's worried about her…. They're friends," she thought to add, not sure if Paul wanted the world to know about his interest in Vivien. She wondered if Alex would believe they were just friends. After all, he'd seen Vivien on several occasions dangling from Paul's arm like a leech.

But Alex didn't question her about it. "I'd hate for you to take on Vivien *and* her mother alone. They may sick their dogs on you. Want some company?"

After letting a twice-masked Ellen know where they were going, they checked in briefly at the Longwell house. Both patients were sleeping, though Anna was restless.

Alice and Alex slipped quietly out and into the street. "She looks so tiny and blue," Alex said as they turned a corner.

"I know. I'm glad she made it through the night."

"Maybe I could watch her tonight," Alex offered. "You can't stay up another whole night. You look terrible."

"Thank you so much, sir," Alice replied with a little curtsey. "Just what a woman wants to hear."

"What woman? I don't see any woman." He smiled and jumped out of the way of Alice's swiping palm. Looking around the quiet street he added, "I don't see anyone around but little old you and me."

Becoming serious again she said, "It is awfully quiet for a Friday."

A chill ran down her spine. No children played in the yards. No ice trucks made their cold deliveries. No model Ts rumbled past. Just Alice and Alex. Were they crazy to be outside?

Panicky thoughts chased each other through Alice's mind. Preoccupied by worries for her family, friends, the entire city, she almost walked right past Vivien's elegant house. She stopped abruptly and turned to open the short black iron gate to Vivien's immense yard.

Two steps up the walkway to the enormous house, she looked up at the Davenports' massive oak doors. White crepe paper fluttered in the breeze.

# Chapter Thirteen

Alice grabbed Alex's arm to keep from toppling onto the Davenports' stone walkway. She peered again at the massive oak door, wondering if her eyes had deceived her. Ivory crepe still clung to the ornately carved door posts. Had the flu dared to cross that marble threshold?

"Oh, Alex. What should we do?"

Alex stood statue still. Silent. Staring.

Alice whispered, "I feel terrible…saying and thinking all those frightful things about Vivien, when the whole time she may have been…dead."

Alex's voice finally worked. "She may be alive…she may be alive and as nasty as she's always been. I hate the way she treats you, Alice." His fists balled up.

"Me, too…but she didn't deserve to die. What will I tell Paul?"

"You don't know anything to tell him yet. We don't know who died." Vivien had a younger brother, Clifford.

Icy terror filled Alice's veins, freezing her to the spot. She had to find out, for Paul. Before she lost her nerve she said, "Come on." She forced herself to step forward, tugging Alex along behind her by the arm.

"Wait," Alex said, pulling his arm free. "Are you going to talk to Mrs. Davenport?"

"If Vivien's…not there. Do you have a better idea?"

Alice would rather have fought an angry bear or knocked down a hornet's nest than approach Mrs. Davenport. But what else could she do? "You don't have to come with me," she offered, hoping he wouldn't listen.

Alex kicked at the lush manicured lawn. "I'll go."

They climbed the wide steps and Alice rapped the knocker three times. She felt four inches tall standing in front of the imposing door.

Locks scraped and the great door opened. The butler stood stiffly in the marble floored entryway. A chandelier dangled from far above his head and a staircase curved elegantly to the floor above.

"May I help you?" His voice was firm, but kind.

Alice's breath caught in her throat. "Um...I'm...um..." She started again. "Vivien...I'm looking for Vivien."

"I'm afraid Miss Vivien has passed, Miss."

"Oh—no."

"The influenza took her last week."

Loud footsteps echoed in the chamber, growing louder.

"Williams!" called a piercing voice. "Williams, who is at the door?" Mrs. Davenport appeared behind her butler. She was dressed from head to toe in black velvet. Her hair was piled in fancy ringlets atop her head, but was falling down in places and her eyes were puffy.

Mrs. Davenport glared through her swollen eyelids. "You!" she fairly shrieked as if she'd found a rat on the porch.

"Mrs. Davenport," Alice said quietly, "we're sorry to hear about Vivien. I hope Clifford is well."

Ignoring Alice's condolence, Mrs. Davenport coldly asked, "What brings you here?"

"My brother Paul. He was worried about Vivien." Alice's legs shook.

"Tell that Paul," Mrs. Davenport spat his name out, "to mind his own business. Now, please leave."

Anger rose in Alice's throat. Alex grabbed her elbow and subtly shook his head before Alice could regret what she said.

Alice counted to ten to calm herself and gather her courage. Swallowing her rising fury and nerves, she asked, "Did Vivien say anything about Paul? Or leave any letters for him before she..." Her voice trailed off.

"I don't see as that's any of your concern. This family will have no further dealings with him." She stared down her long slender nose at Alice. "Or his relation. Now leave my property, immediately." Mrs. Davenport flicked her hand at them like she was swatting away a pesky fly.

Simultaneously Alice and Alex turned and took the porch steps two at a time. At the bottom step, Alice suddenly turned back to the closing door. She called up the steps, "I know you're grieving, Mrs. Davenport. I'm sorry for your loss. But that's no reason to be rude.

Paul cared for Vivien."

Alice thought she caught a glimmer of humanity, of sadness instead of rage, in those steely eyes before the door firmly shut her outside. She and Alex nearly ran to the gate. Alex fumbled quickly with the latch and Alice slammed the gate closed behind them. The pair ran through the silent streets all the way home.

Alice returned her pen to the inkwell and blew on her words to Paul to dry the ink. This letter had been painful to write, but after a good night's sleep she had been up to the task.

Their encounter with Mrs. Davenport had drained Alice of any strength she had had. She had lain on the porch swing for several hours, talking with Alex about Vivien, the flu, and the letter to Paul. Ellen had appeared at the window several times, but amazingly had not insisted Alice come inside and help her. Weakness and numbness had soaked into Alice's bones and she hoped her weariness was only caused by her night watching Anna and the visit with Mrs. Davenport. Was this how people felt when the flu first attacked their bodies?

After their talk, Alex had insisted Alice go to bed and get some rest. He would take Mama's place as the Longwells' nurse. "After all, I'm their neighbor too." Alice had not had the energy to refuse.

Now she slipped the newly addressed letter to Paul into her dress pocket and darted down the stairs, energy renewed.

Ellen stood at the stove, stirring oatmeal with one hand and bouncing a whining Caleb on her hip. She gave an exhausted look to Alice over her double mask.

"Good morning, Ellen," Alice said. She flew through the kitchen, stopping only to pat Caleb on the back and grab a biscuit off the stove. Her hand was on the doorknob when Ellen asked, "Where are you going?"

"To check on Anna and Mrs. Longwell."

"And leave me here again with Ben and Caleb and all the chores? Mama's already gone over."

She lifted Caleb off her hip and thrust him at Alice.

"Mama," Caleb said with a whimper.

"He's been asking for her all morning," Ellen complained.

"Actually he's been saying that for two days, but I guess you wouldn't know that, now would you?"

"Sorry, Ellen," Alice said, sitting down at the table to bounce Caleb on her knee.

Ellen continued. "I left you alone on the porch yesterday because you looked so tired. But now I need you. I can't do all the housework and care for two children." Ellen stirred the oatmeal vigorously.

Ben shuffled into the kitchen, lip quivering. "I'm your helper."

Ellen put her hand to her mask. She lifted the oatmeal off the burner and stooped to Ben's level. "You're right, Ben. I mispoke. We take care of Caleb together. You are my helper."

Ben thrust his mask at Ellen and she tied it over his mouth as she talked to him. "Please take Caleb into the parlor and play blocks with him while I make breakfast."

Alice plopped Caleb onto his pudgy legs and Ben took his hand. "Ugh. Sticky! Why is he always sticky?" As they left the room Ben told Caleb, "You better not throw the blocks this time. I mean it!"

Alice stood.

Ellen clanked the oatmeal pot back onto the heat and glared at Alice.

Alice stared back, defiantly. "I'll hurry back." Anna was more important than a tidy house. "The Longwells need us."

"There was enough to do around here before you went off to find other people's problems."

"What did you want me to do," Alice asked, her voice rising, "leave a sick mother with her two toddlers all alone? Maybe I should have just ordered three coffins and left them all to die."

Ellen collapsed in a chair, laid her head in her arms, and cried. Alice went to Ellen and stroked her back.

"I'm sorry, Ellen. I shouldn't have said that."

Ellen lifted her head and brushed away a tear. "No, that's just it. You're right. I'm being selfish. I know we need to help the Longwells. It's just that I'm so tired. And I'm so scared. When is this going to end?"

"I don't know. I'm tired and scared, too."

"You don't act scared."

"Well, I am," Alice said. "Every minute."

"I worry every time Ben seems warm, Father coughs, or I'm

tired."

"I worry, too. I can't believe Mrs. Schneider's gone. And Vivien—she was *our* age."

Silence filled the kitchen. Who else their age would be forever missing when they finally returned to school. Alice pictured empty desks dotting her classroom.

Ellen smoothed her hair and stood. "You go. I'll be fine."

"Are you sure?"

"Positive."

Alice gave Ellen a quick hug, grabbed her biscuit off the table, and headed for the door. "I'll be back as soon as I can."

As she devoured her biscuit and walked through the dewy grass in the chilly October air, Alice could hear Ben in the kitchen saying, "He hit me in the head with a block!" She shook her head and wondered how much more Ellen could take. Ellen had always been so strong, so in control. But this epidemic was getting to everybody. Alice quickened her step.

Alex was slipping out the front door as Alice reached the Longwells' porch.

"Morning," Alice said.

"Morning, Alice." Alex rubbed a bleary eye.

"Thanks for taking my place. How are the patients?"

"Mrs. Longwell's on the mend. Anna tossed and turned all night, but she's sleeping now."

"Good. Thought I'd stop in and see them."

"All right. Your mama just arrived." Alex kicked at a wayward leaf on the porch. It skidded across the wood, then landed softly on the others in the grass. "Did you write Paul?"

"Yep." She pulled the letter out of her pocket. "I hate to mail him such bad news."

"He asked you to find out about Vivien. He needs to know. I would want to know…" Alex paused, kicked at another leaf, then continued. "I worry about my father all the time. Every day I worry that we'll get a telegram telling us he's been killed. I never want to get that telegram, but if something bad has happened to him, I want to know. Paul wants to know, too. And he trusts you to tell him."

He gently pried the letter from Alice's hand. "I'll mail this at the store for you."

Alice felt the now familiar shiver as Alex's strong hand brushed her petite one. "Thank you."

Alex took the porch steps two at a time, then turned in the grass. "See you soon, I hope. I'll rest a bit, then Mama needs me. She's worn out from all this extra work, too."

"I'm sure she is. Tell her I said 'hello.' And thanks again, Alex."

"Sure, Alice." He took a few backward steps, then turned and strode toward home.

As Alex's form disappeared behind her house, Alice looked into the robin's egg blue sky. Puffy cotton clouds floated by, oblivious to the pain and heartache down below. Alice longed to join the clouds in their carefree flight. A ragged cough from inside the house pinned her back to earth.

# Chapter Fourteen

Saturday, Sunday, and Monday were a blur of cooking, cleaning, caring for Anna, entertaining Caleb and Ben, and praying that this nightmare would soon be over. Everywhere she turned, Alice found something needing to be done or someone needing her attention. Even with Father's help entertaining the children on Sunday, the work never seemed to stop.

"Alice, will you come here please?" Ellen's impatient voice dragged Alice from the clothes she was folding on the kitchen table to the front parlor. Caleb was squealing and squirming from Ellen's arms while Ben sat on the piano bench crying, holding his favorite book, *Aesop's Fables*, in one hand and several torn pages in the other.

"He ruined it, Alice," Ben sobbed, pointing at Caleb.

Sitting down on the bench next to Ben, Alice put her arm around him and said, "I can try to glue it, Ben. It will be okay."

"It won't be okay," Ben whined.

Ben's whine showed Alice how much he needed to get away from Caleb for awhile. She could use a break herself. They'd been cooped up together too long.

"Why don't I take Ben out for a walk?" Alice offered. Ben's eyes got big. He was probably thinking of their last walk together.

Ellen was obviously at her wit's end for she agreed to Alice's suggestion. Ben's eyes grew even larger. Ellen said, "I can't stand these two together anymore. Ben's so particular about everything and Caleb's determined to destroy anything he gets his hands on." Caleb yanked on Ellen's hair as if proving her point. She disentangled his pudgy, gooey fingers. "Ow!"

In a flash Alice kissed Caleb's hair, gave her sister a quick sideways hug, and scooted out the door, pulling Ben along behind her.

"Put your mask on," Ellen called from the doorway. Alice pulled the crumpled piece of cloth from her pocket and tied it on. Ellen,

Ben, and Caleb wore their masks all the time, but Alice couldn't stand it and took it off every chance she got.

"Come on, Ben, this will be fun!" Alice said, dragging Ben down the street.

"Will not," Ben said, twisting his captured arm one way, then the other. A button popped from his sleeve. It bounced off the brick road, then settled in a crack, next to a brown leaf. Ben scurried to retrieve his button and jammed it deep into his pants pocket. "Now look what you did. This isn't fun at all." He examined his shirt sleeve flopping open in the fall breeze.

Alice pulled the red ribbon from her hair and stooped to tie it around Ben's sleeve, holding it closed. "Ben, if you really don't want to come I'll take you back home. Do you want to spend the afternoon with Caleb or with me?"

Ben fiddled with the ribbon as he thought. "You, I guess. You never play with me anymore."

"I am today. Now, why don't we see if Alex can come along with us?"

"Okay."

Alex wasn't at home so the two headed to Becks' General Store, hoping Alex would have a few minutes to spend with them. Business was slow, so Alex slipped off his apron and waved good-bye to his mama.

The threesome jostled each other down the near empty street. It was good to be outside in the fresh town air without adult responsibilities. Ben seemed to have forgotten his earlier jitters and was happily kicking a stone down the street.

But they could not get too far from the epidemic and the war. Alice read signs posting epidemic hours in several store windows. A poster nailed to a pole told her to "buy war bonds." "Closed" signs hung on pool hall, bowling alley, and tavern doors which were closed because of the epidemic. The tavern and pool hall windows were blank staring eyes where laughter and light used to poor out.

Still, Alice was determined to keep the mood cheerful.

"Race you!" she dared the boys.

"Down to McGuffey's Pool Hall," Alex said, taking up the challenge.

"Ben, you run down to the end of the block for your head start."

"But I'll get dirty..." Ben started. Alice gave him an exasperated look. "Oh, okay." Kicking his rock all the way, Ben hurried, as fast as he ever hurried, to the next block.

"Ready, set, go!" Alice yelled and the three were off. Their cheers and footsteps echoed through the abandoned streets. By the end of their third block, Alice and Alex had caught up with Ben and the three were running neck in neck for the pool hall.

Alice picked up speed and tagged the building's corner just ahead of Alex's outstretched hand.

"I...won!" Alice said between gasps of air. She leaned against a barrel outside the pool hall to catch her breath. Laughing between breaths, Ben collapsed against the barrel and Alex joined him.

"Ben! Aren't you worried about getting your clothes dirty on the filthy ground?" Alice asked, amazed.

"They'll wash," Ben replied. "I'm too tired to stand right now."

"Me, too," Alex said and tousled Ben's hair. Ben started to protest, then smiled.

"Uh oh," Alice teased. "I think Ben's caught a sloppy bug."

"Did not catch a sloppy bug," Ben protested. "I didn't catch any bugs at all today—just one lousy crawdad—and I let him go."

Alex and Alice laughed, while Ben looked confused.

Suddenly they grew quiet. Laughter and piano music rang through the air. Men's voices.

"It's coming from the pool hall," Alice whispered. "Look, the lights are on."

Suddenly the laughter changed to shouting and the tinkling piano melody was replaced by the sounds of shattering glass and loud thuds. Alice and Alex slowly crept toward the yellow lamplight spilling into the alley between the pool hall and the fabric store next to it. Silently, slowly they rose from the dirt until they could see over the dusty window-sill into the room. They couldn't believe the scene that met their eyes.

# Chapter Fifteen

Alice ducked with Alex as a pitcher flew toward the pool hall window. It shattered against the wall, inches from the glass. Alice screamed, startled. Alex put his hand over her masked mouth.

They rose again to peer into the room. Alice had passed pool halls before and even stared into a window of one once, before Ellen had yanked her away. She had seen men playing cards and pool, laughing, eating, and drinking. The men here may have come to have a good time, but the room looked anything but fun now. Near the window a man was sprawled on a pool table protecting himself from another man's swings. Two men were dueling with cue sticks. Fist fights were breaking out in every corner and tables and chairs were flung on their sides. Playing cards and water, or was it beer, littered the floor along with several unlucky patrons. Several men were briskly heading for the doors. Several policemen swung billy clubs in every direction, trying to control the mob.

Alice and Alex crouched again as a man was tossed against the window.

Alex whispered loudly over the din. "They're getting arrested for breaking quarantine! Let's get out of here."

"Just a minute." Alice peeked over the window-sill again. As a policeman pulled a man to his feet, he glanced toward the window. Alice dropped to the dirt.

The city had closed pool halls and other unnecessary businesses to keep people from spreading the flu to each other. Still, it seemed a bit harsh to be arrested for playing cards.

"Let's go!" Alex insisted. "I don't wanna go to jail!"

"You won't. We're not breaking quarantine just by being in town."

"I guess. But we're supposed to stay away from people. There's an awful lot of people here. Any one of them could have the flu."

Alice cautiously got onto her knees and brushed dust off her dress. "Wonder why they were fighting," she whispered loudly.

Alex crouched, balancing on his toes. "Probably edgy because they were afraid of getting caught."

"Or afraid they'd catch the flu from someone."

As they spoke two men darted from the back alley and disappeared around the corner of the fabric store. A policeman chased after the escapees, billy club raised. Alice and Alex flattened themselves against the building.

No one had come near them. They should be safe from the flu. But could they be arrested? Alice wasn't really sure. The quarantine rules were awfully strict. She could get arrested just for littering. No one knew how the Spanish flu spread, but trash was a suspect. Why, if the war hadn't sent most of the young men to Europe, they probably would have hired extra men to be litter police. That would be a great job for neatnik Ben. Ben!

"Alex, where's Ben?"

Alex glanced down the brick wall of the building. "He must have stayed over by the barrel."

Alex and Alice rushed back to the barrel, but it stood alone against the pool hall wall. Panic surged through Alice's body. "You look around back. I'll take the front of the building." Alice ran around the corner, nearly running into the row of men leaving the pool hall and entering the paddy wagon. She darted around the barred wagon and around the building. Alex jogged around the back corner, Ben-less.

"Where could he have gone?" Alice asked, frantic.

"I'm sure he's not far."

"Let's go down the street toward your store—the way we came."

Alice and Alex zig-zagged down the street, checking behind trash barrels, in alleys, and under stands of products for sale.

"Ben, Ben where are you?"

Shop doors stood open to let in the fall breezes, cooling the stores as well as blowing disease away. Alice stopped in the first one she came to—"Frazier Fabrics."

The shop walls were lined with bolts of cloth and bins of notions. Alice hurried up to the clerk who was carefully measuring yellow calico for her only customer. Both ladies looked up, startled.

"Have you seen a six-year-old boy with brown hair?"

"No, hun. This isn't a shop for little boys. You might try the toy store down the street."

"Thank you," Alice called as she dashed out the door.

But the toy store's doors were locked and windows dark. A sign informed customers that there was illness in the family. Alice and Alex rushed from store to store, but found no Ben. At each store the shopkeepers and meager collection of shoppers said they hadn't seen him or just shook their masked downcast heads. He wasn't even at the fire station or the bookstore, two places he loved.

They passed a little house amongst the businesses. Four small children danced in a ring in the tiny front yard. Alice stopped, mesmerized. The children's sing-songy voices chanted:

*I had a little bird*
*Her name was Enza*
*I opened the window*
*And in-flu-enza.*

They chanted the verse over and over, like a tinny, disturbing music box. Alice couldn't look away. Finally, the touch of Alex's hand on her arm broke the spell and the two went on to the bakery next door.

Alice's dread rose as the minutes ticked by. What if they couldn't find him? What if he had collapsed in an alley and couldn't hear their calls? "And in-flew-enza" danced through her mind.

Wild stories filled Alice's head. A woman, upset because her little boy was killed by the influenza, stole Ben to replace her lost child. No, she was crazy with her loss, and thought Ben *was* her little boy. She was stroking his hair and calling him Patrick or Joseph right this minute. Alice quickened her steps and called louder, "Ben, Ben where are you?"

As they reached the Becks' store Alice sat down hard on the curb and dropped her head into her cradled arms. They were blocks and blocks from the pool hall and there was no sign of Ben.

Alex said, "We'll find him," then dashed inside the store calling, "Mama, Mama have you seen Ben?"

Alice heard rustling behind her. She turned toward a wooden

table covered with pumpkins and squash. Underneath the table, between two crates of vegetables, two large eyes peered out of a tear-stained, dirty face. The face sniffled.

"Ben?" Could that unruly mop of curls really belong to Ben? Spotting her red ribbon dangling from the boy's sleeve she cried, "Ben!"

Tentatively, Ben crawled out of his hiding place into the dimming afternoon light. Alice squeezed him tightly, then held him at arm's length. His left sleeve was torn from shoulder to cuff, but he didn't look hurt, just scared.

Alice said. "You had us worried to death."

"Men were chasing me!"

"What men?"

"Men from the pool hall. They came by the barrel and I was scared. So I ran as fast as I could. They chased me."

"Are you sure they were chasing you? They were probably just running away from the policemen."

"I didn't ask them," Ben said.

Alice laughed, her worry melting away. She hugged him again.

Alex came to the doorway followed by Mrs. Beck.

"You found him!" Alex said.

"I'm so glad," Mrs. Beck added. She looked the usually spotless Ben up and down. "Your clothes! Your face!" She swiped at his dirty face with a corner of her apron.

"I hid under the pumpkins. I think a nail tore my shirt." He fingered his torn sleeve.

"I'm sure your mama can mend that," Mrs. Beck said, smiling as she examined the ripped material.

A lump crept into Alice throat. Mama. And Father. And Ellen. She'd be punished for sure this time.

# Chapter Sixteen

Upon arriving home, Alice explained the afternoon in town to Mama who was briefly home making soup for the Longwells. Mama dropped her wooden spoon and examined Ben from head to toe with exhausted fingers.

"I'm fine, Mama. Really," Ben said. A welcome change from the whiny tattling. Alice smiled slightly at Ben and he smiled back over Mama's shoulder as she examined his legs.

After sending Ben to change into unripped clothes, Mama turned to Alice.

"When will you learn?"

Alice remained silent, knowing Mama did not expect an answer. She fiddled with a cool porcelain drawer knob and stared out the kitchen window at the falling darkness.

"Look at me when I'm speaking to you."

Alice pulled her gaze from the distant silhouetted trees to Mama's near, angry eyes.

"I didn't mean to lose Ben."

"I realize that. But we need you to be more responsible. Especially in times like these."

"I'll do better. I promise."

"You won't make such a mistake any time soon." She turned to Alice. "It seems that the only way to keep you out of trouble is to keep you here. Until further notice you will spend your days in your room, mending. The mending's been neglected and the pile's high as a hay stack."

Mending? Mending was the worst chore ever, even worse than knitting. A whipping would be better. Over and done with.

"And you will not see Alex." Alice sunk into a chair. For how long?

As Mama gathered supplies for the Longwells she gave her final instructions. "Make dinner, then off to bed. Maybe an empty stomach will help you realize the folly of your ways."

Alice felt her stomach rumble as she opened the ice box and took out the milk bottle to make biscuits for dinner.

After a hungry Tuesday night, Alice spent Wednesday confined to her bedroom with the haystack of clothes to mend. She began with Ben's torn shirt and missing button.

Several hours later, as she battled one of Paul's stubborn frayed collars, she heard a soft knock. Ben walked slowly into the room and sat on the edge of the bed, making it bounce and creak.

"Sorry, Alice."

Alice stuck the needle through the shirt's fabric and looked up at Ben.

"Sorry for what?"

"I got you in trouble. I shouldn't have run away from those men."

"You didn't mean to get me in trouble." She couldn't stop herself from adding, "Like you do sometimes."

"You're always doing wild stuff," he complained. "I usually hate that. But yesterday…"

"What?"

"It was sort of fun."

Alice smiled.

"Do you need any help?" Ben asked.

"When did you learn how to mend?"

"You could teach me."

"I think Ellen would appreciate your help with Caleb."

"But you're all alone up here. Besides, Caleb's sticky."

"Watching Caleb's way more fun than mending." Alice jabbed the needle into the collar. And her finger. "Ouch!" She stuck her bleeding finger into her mouth.

"That's what you think. He didn't rip *your* book."

"Yes, he did. *Aesop's Fables* is our family's book, not just yours." Alice had loved those stories since before Ben was even born.

Ben asked, "What's your favorite story?"

"'The Lion and the Mouse.'"

"Mine, too. I like how the mouse helps the lion even though the mouse is little like me."

Alice tousled Ben's hair and said, "Well, little mouse, I think it's time for you to play with Caleb. I hear him crying downstairs."

Ben hopped off the bed, waved good-bye to Alice, and clomped down the stairs.

Little creatures could help even with big problems. She wondered if that was true with a problem as large as an influenza epidemic.

In the afternoon, Miss Lang dropped by, saving Alice from dying of boredom. With school being closed, Miss Lang and other teachers had been spending their free time visiting families, selling war bonds, and giving out information about the flu. Despite Ellen's disapproving glances, Alice extended the visit for as long as possible, enjoying the mending break and Miss Lang's company. A cough and tired eyes reminded Alice how terribly sick Miss Lang had been.

Miss Lang handed Alice a pamphlet entitled, "Spanish Influenza." She managed to read a few suggestions for avoiding the flu before Caleb toddled over and ripped off the top half. Chew food carefully. Wash hands often. Get fresh air…. Alice thought, "When I get fresh air I get trouble right along with it." She pressed her needle-pricked index finger. Ow.

Miss Lang shared influenza cures she'd heard about, like people wearing bags of garlic-scented gum around their necks. She had even heard of people wearing necklaces of chicken feathers and had a neighbor who stuck an ace of diamonds in his shoe to keep the flu away.

"Did it work?" Alice asked.

"Well, no. He fell sick yesterday." A silent chill filled the room.

Alice told Miss Lang she'd heard of people covering sick loved ones in chopped onions and others who swore by eating lemons. No one knew if these "cures" did any good, but anything was worth a try. Mama had concocted her own "medicine" for the Longwells. Alice wasn't sure of the ingredients, but she knew it contained kerosene and smelled awful.

After Miss Lang's call, Alice trudged back upstairs. The pile of torn and worn clothes slowly shrank as the mended clothes pile grew. Still, there was plenty of sewing to keep Alice busy another day or two. How did six people wear out so many clothes? She'd make a point to be more careful in the future, she thought, patching the threadbare elbow on her red calico dress.

After dinner Alice got another short break from sewing. Father read the newspaper and allowed Alice to stay and listen. In a short article the paper reported that five men had been arrested for breaking quarantine by assembling in a pool hall to play pool and cards.

"Those are the men we saw!" Ben said excitedly.

"There were a lot more, but they got away," Alice added, feeling proud to have witnessed something that actually appeared in the newspaper.

Father said, "Those men were foolish. I hope their families don't suffer for their afternoon of fun."

After dinner Alice patched two pairs of Father's pants by lamplight, changed into her nightgown, and climbed into bed. Her hands ached and her eyes burned like she'd gotten smoke in them. She dreaded tomorrow's monotony of patching knees and reattaching buttons. And the socks. Darning socks all day was enough to drive any person insane.

Alice woke to a knock at the bedroom door. The room was dim with the beginnings of morning. Ellen didn't stir beside her so Alice rose to answer. Mama stood in the hallway, dressed and ready for the day.

Her words were quiet, but sounded loud in the morning stillness. "Normally you'd be confined to this house for quite awhile, young lady, after your behavior, but these are trying times. I need you."

Alice worked hard to contain a smile.

Mama continued, "The Longwells still require nursing but your grandpa must have a visit as well."

Today was Thursday! Grandpa visiting day! Maybe Mama would let her care for the Longwells while she was gone. No mending!

But Mama's news was even better than Alice had hoped. She and Alex would be visiting Grandpa instead of Mama. Mama wanted to keep Alice away from the Longwells' influenza and Mrs. Beck could spare Alex for one day.

Mama continued, "No matter what your father says, Grandpa is certainly not okay by himself in that apartment of his. He needs help and some company. Now hurry. Get yourself dressed and meet me downstairs in ten minutes."

"I will, Mama. And, thank you. I won't let you down."

"I know you won't, dear." She gave Alice a quick smile, then turned toward the stairs. "Ten minutes," she called over her shoulder.

Alice was ready in five.

# Chapter Seventeen

Within half an hour Alex and Alice were jostling along in the trolley toward downtown. Alice held a picnic basket in her lap, filled with canned goods, bread, and biscuits for Grandpa, as well as sandwiches, apples, and a list of instructions. They watched carefully for their stop and hopped off the car.

Alice looked around at the three- and four-story buildings surrounding them. She had been to Grandpa's apartment many times, but always with Mama or Father. Realizing now that she had never paid close attention to how to get there, she pulled out Mama's directions. "Grandpa's apartment should be two blocks south," Alice told Alex, pointing. As they walked, Alice compared the building numbers with Mama's spidery writing until the two matched.

They climbed the steps and Alex pulled open one of the two large glass doors. The lobby was dimly lit by gas wall lamps. The large flowery area rug in the center of the room was worn, but clean. Dark, polished wood paneled the room and one wall was lined with little gold mailboxes with tiny keyholes.

After climbing the three flights of stairs, Alice knocked on door 412. There was no answer. She knocked again. Muffled noises seemed to be coming from inside, but still Grandpa did not come to the door.

Alice called, "Grandpa, it's me, Alice. Are you in there?"

More soft sounds like knocking and soft calls drifted through the door. Alice couldn't make out the words.

"I'm coming in, Grandpa," she called through the door. Handing Alex the basket to free her hands, Alice slipped a pink ribbon from around her neck. Dangling from the ribbon was a shiny gold key—in case of an emergency, Mama had said. Alice slid the key into the lock, felt and heard it click open. She replaced the key around her neck and turned the handle.

The ticktock of Grandpa's wall clock rhythmically interrupted the silence that hung in the shadowy parlor. Years of Grandpa's pipe smoke filled every corner with its sweet odor.

"Grandpa?"

A raspy voice answered from the right. Alice darted around the rocking chair and into the yellow walled kitchen. She gasped. Grandpa was laying in the middle of a puddle of water on the floor, his right leg bent under him at a curious angle.

"Glory be, child, am I glad to see you!" Grandpa croaked.

Alice rushed over to him and knelt. "What happened to you, Grandpa?"

"This newfangled contraption, that's what happened to me," he said, pointing a shaky finger at the ice box, leaking onto the kitchen floor.

Alice grabbed a towel and began mopping the cold water away from Grandpa.

"Never should have allowed such a thing in my home," Grandpa continued, "but your grandma had her heart set on one, God rest her soul."

Alice smoothed Grandpa's pearl-white hair away from his wrinkled face.

Grandpa pushed her hand away. "It ain't my hair that hurts. It's my leg. That durn ice box's been leaking all over your grandma's kitchen floor. So I tried to fix it and look at the thanks I get. Slipped in this cold puddle."

He rubbed his bent leg and groaned.

"Is it broken?" Alex asked, stooping next to Grandpa.

"Which, the ice box or my leg? Both, I think."

"We have to get you to the hospital right away!" Alice said. She grabbed him under the arms and tugged, trying to get him off the floor. Grandpa pressed himself to the floor, like Caleb when he didn't want to go to bed.

"No, siree. I'm not going to one of those influenza death traps. My leg's broke, not my mind. Go to one of them hospitals and you'll come out sicker'n when you went in. If you come out at all."

"But we have no choice, Grandpa," Alice protested, sounding like her mother to her ears. "Your leg is broken and they can fix it so it mends straight."

"I'll do just fine with the help of you two young'uns. If you promise we'll stay right here at home I'll get up with your help."

Grandpa needed a hospital, but he also needed to be off the floor. Reluctantly she promised.

Grandpa smiled. "We're in business. And none too soon. I've been laying in this puddle all day and I'm about to make a new one of my own." He cackled at his own joke then groaned again.

Alice surveyed the room, then pulled a kitchen chair behind Grandpa. "Alex, you get one arm, I'll get the other." With a lot of muscle from Alice and Alex and a lot of grunting from Grandpa, they managed to get him onto the chair.

"See, I'm better already," Grandpa said through gritted teeth. "You two beat the hospital any day."

"You don't look better," Alice protested. Grandpa's foot stuck out from his calf like the bottom of a capital 'L.' His face looked like he'd eaten a whole crate of lemons.

"Now, we've got to get to the water closet. That's one newfangled contraption that's mighty handy."

Alex and Alice scooted, dragged, and carried the wooden chair holding Grandpa from the kitchen to the water closet. They tried to protect Grandpa's injured leg as much as possible, but by the look on Grandpa's face, they weren't doing a very good job. Still, he didn't make a peep. He probably realized that too much moaning would wind him up in the hospital. Alice would drag him there if he looked like he was in too much pain. She'd inherited his stubborn streak.

Alex helped Grandpa while Alice searched the large, oak wardrobe for some dry clothes. After what seemed like hours they had Grandpa settled in the rocker in dry clothes.

"Now," Grandpa said gruffly. "I need you two to straighten the break."

"What?" Alice said.

"It has to be done, Alice, or the leg will never heal," Alex said.

"Smart boy," Grandpa said. "You oughta hang on to this one, Alice. He'll make a good husband."

Alice blushed. She started to protest, then stopped herself. Maybe Grandpa could plant the idea in Alex's mind if it wasn't there already.

"Oh, Grandpa," she said.

"I'll hold onto the chair arms and you pull my leg straight, Alex. Alice, you hold onto the back of the chair so it doesn't move. Get in place and I'll count to three."

"Wait," Alice said. "We can't do this. It'll hurt too much."

"Back in the War between the States men had their wounded legs sawed off and lived through the pain. I think I can manage."

Alice hesitated, then took her position behind the chair. Grasping the chair, she braced her feet. As Alex pulled, she held her breath. Grandpa let out a cry, but the bone remained stubbornly crooked.

"Try...again," Grandpa gasped, tears forming in his eyes.

"No, Grandpa," Alice said. "We can't do this alone. If you won't let us take you to the hospital, at least let me get some help."

Grandpa was quiet a moment, then said, "Myles Price is a good chap. Wife was a nurse before they had their young'un. He works nights, so he should be home with the missus. Apartment 416."

Alice sprinted out the door, found 416, and knocked loudly.

A young woman answered the door, pretty brown curls surrounding her stark white mask. She bounced a masked baby on her hip.

Alice explained the situation and Mrs. Price called to her husband. The whole family rushed with Alice to Grandpa's aid, Mr. Price tucking in a shirt and donning suspenders as he ran.

Alice and Mrs. Price held Grandpa and the chair in place, while Alex and Mr. Price braced themselves to pull the leg. "One, two, three, pull." Alex and Mr. Price yanked, tumbling backwards onto Grandma's rag rug. Grandpa yelped as his leg bone snapped into place.

Taking Grandpa's white knuckled hand Alice asked, "Are you all right, Grandpa?"

"I've had better moments, but, yes, I'm all right." He gave her a weak smile and patted her arm. He closed his eyes for several minutes.

"Now if we want it to stay straight, we need some sort of splint," Mrs. Price said, keeping an eye on the baby who was trying to roll over on the rug.

Alice and Alex searched the apartment for something to hold the leg in place and came back with a shelf from the wardrobe. The group huddled over their patient, attaching the shelf to the back of Grandpa's leg with strips of cloth. Alice found Grandma's old cane and laid it next to the chair.

Grandpa closed his eyes again, as if willing the pain to go away. The baby cooed loudly and Alice turned to watch the infant try to fit her entire hand in her mouth.

Alice turned back to Grandpa, wondering if he'd fallen asleep. He opened one blue eye and asked Alice, "Did you bring any grub?"

"Yes, Grandpa. Are you hungry? We brought sandwiches, apples, biscuits…"

"Don't just talk about it, serve it up. Now that I'm up off that wet floor and my leg doesn't look like a bent twig, my stomach's complaining something fierce. Haven't eaten since supper yesterday."

"We'll be going now," Mr. Price said. "I'll stop by to check on you before I leave for work."

"Hogwash. Stay for lunch. We have plenty, don't we, Alice?"

"Plenty. Please stay."

The couple looked at each other, then Mr. Price said, "Much obliged. To tell the truth it'd be nice to visit."

Alice and Mrs. Price prepared the food, adding pickles and stewed tomatoes from Grandpa's cupboard to Mama's basket of food. They discussed the baby, the flu and the war. Mrs. Price was worried that Mr. Price would be drafted. Alice told her about Paul joining up.

"Myles wants to go. Many of his friends joined up or were drafted, but he knows he's needed here now that we have little Mary. And the police force is glad to have him. Most of the younger officers are off fighting."

"I'll never understand why men want to go off to war."

"I suppose it's because they care about us. They want their families to be safe."

"I guess you're right," Alice said, pride and warmth filling her heart. Paul was willing to risk his life to keep her safe. What a great big brother. According to his last letter, he'd be shipping out very soon. She hoped he'd be safe.

Alice and Mary carted the food out to the parlor so Grandpa didn't have to move. Alice handed Grandpa his plate of food and sat down on the rag rug close to baby Mary. Everyone removed their masks, said grace, and began to eat.

Mr. Price asked Grandpa about his accident with the ice box and promised to take a look at it after lunch.

"The puddle's cleaned up for now," Alice said. "And I put what was left of the ice back in the ice box."

"Thank you, child. I sure do appreciate all your help today."

"Well, you did me a favor too, Grandpa," Alice said and continued with an account of the past two days.

Unlike Mama, Father, and Ellen, Grandpa laughed at the story. He shook his head. "That Benny. What a character. And you're quite a character yourself, little lady. Always getting into one scrape or another. You're a lot like your grandpa." He smiled fondly.

They spent the early afternoon telling stories. Grandpa told about his boyhood years in Cincinnati, his time in the Union army, and his years with Grandma. Alice had heard these stories before, but enjoyed the retelling nevertheless. Plus, Grandpa's pain seemed to lessen as he talked.

Mr. Price told police stories. The day before he had had to arrest two men for brawling in the street. One man punched the other in the face for breathing on him.

Alex said, "We had a customer yesterday who refused to buy wheat flour, after a little boy coughed in the dry goods aisle. He wasn't even near the flour bins."

"This flu has people acting crazy," Mr. Price concluded.

"I know. My sister, Ellen, wears two masks at a time, and refuses to leave the house."

Grandpa said, "That Ellen's a smart one. Wear masks. Keep to your house. That's the best way to prevent the sickness."

"But if we had done that," Alice protested, "we wouldn't have come here. You would have been on the floor for who knows how long, and I would have been mending shirts until I went blind."

"And we wouldn't have had this enjoyable afternoon," Mrs. Price added, holding sleeping Mary.

"That's true, too. I'm glad Alice had the spunk to visit me or I'd have been in a heap of trouble." He paused. "Well, speaking of trouble, Alice, you don't need any more of it. You two'd better git before they send the posse out looking for you."

Alice and Alex rose. Alice asked, "Will you be okay here, Grandpa?"

"We'll check in on him," said Mr. Price, helping his wife to her feet.

Grandpa said, "I'll be just fine. I have Grandma's cane here beside me and my one good leg. And I have good neighbors." He winked at the Prices. "I'm a clumsy old coot, but I'll be right as rain before you know it." He pushed himself up out of the chair with the cane. It was obvious he was trying not to grimace. "Now off you go…and don't go tellin' your mama about this or she'll be over here quick as a jack rabbit."

Grandpa scooted them out the door.

As they walked toward the trolley stop, Alice debated telling Mama.

"You have to tell your parents," Alex said.

"I guess…I just hate betraying Grandpa."

"He'll understand."

"You don't know Grandpa. If Mama comes, he may not let her in the door."

"He'll let her in. He's hurting more than he's letting on."

"I know he is." Alice couldn't get Grandpa's pain-filled face out of her mind.

# Chapter Eighteen

Mama bustled with activity after Alice arrived home with her bad news about Grandpa. She flew from room to room gathering items she planned to take with her and giving instructions to Ellen and Alice who followed frantically in her wake.

Mama was taking the last trolley that evening to stay with Grandpa, despite Father's protests. He had come home soon after Alice to find Mama packing a bag and telling Alice to check in on the Longwells twice a day to make sure everything was fine.

"What's going on, dear?" Father asked, trying to kiss her forehead as she scurried past him to the wardrobe.

"Your father has broken his leg and I intend to care for him."

"Is he all right?" Father asked.

"Of course he's not all right. He has a broken leg; I just told you that. Alice and Alex did their best to make him comfortable, but he needs someone to do for him until he can get around again. I hate to burden those nice Prices, what with that new baby to care for and those long hours Myles puts in on the police force."

"Why don't we take him to the hospital?"

Mama looked at him incredulously. "You know Father's feelings about hospitals—'you come out sicker'n you went in—if you come out at all,'" she said sounding just like Grandpa.

Alice giggled and Father smiled.

"Besides," Mama said, "with this horrible epidemic, I tend to agree with Grandpa. He's safer at home."

Alice said, "He'll be okay with Mama."

"I'm not worried about your mama's nursing skills," Father said, "she's sure had enough practice lately between rolling bandages for the Red Cross and caring for the Longwells." He caught Mama with one arm as she tried to pass him to get to the dresser. "But, Grace," he said, holding her tightly around the waist. "You can only burn the candle at both ends for so long. You're going to wear yourself out and get sick."

"I feel fine, Walter. Besides, I'll only be gone a couple of days, to get Grandpa settled in comfortably. I know he'd protest a longer stay."

Alice remembered Grandpa's parting words. He'd fight any stay at all, but he needed their help.

Mama continued, "Once I'm home again, he'll have to rely on the Prices some—until my usual Thursday visit, next week."

Father was silent a moment, then said, "I guess a few days won't tire you too terribly, even if they're with my hardheaded father. You're a very special lady, Grace Brockmann!" He gave her a hug and kissed her brazenly on the mouth.

"Walter, the children," Mama protested, Father's lips muffling her words.

When Father finished his kiss he replied, "Better look again. These two aren't children anymore. Not quite women yet, but certainly not children." He smiled, kissed Mama again, and released his hold around her waist

Alice smiled, feeling older inside somehow.

Mama instantly resumed her frenzied packing, sending Ellen scurrying for canned peaches and Alice for bandages.


Within the hour, Mama was climbing the steps of the last trolley of the day, her arms bundled with supplies and her lips calling out last-minute instructions and affections. "See you soon. I'll call the Becks' store from a neighbor's apartment to leave news for you. Give the Becks any messages for me. I'll miss you all," she called to her gathered family. Alice hiked Caleb up on her hip and waved. He followed her lead and waved too. The trolley car rumbled down the street.

Mama was gone. And the corner felt suddenly empty. Alice got a lump in her throat. She had been glad when Mama had insisted on caring for Grandpa, but Mama had never been away before. Even while at the Longwells, she had only been a short walk across the yard if they needed to know the special spice she always put on the chicken, or how to get squealing Caleb to go to sleep.

Alice realized now how much she depended on Mama's just being there. As Alice walked along the street toward home, surrounded by family and holding Caleb's hand, she thought about Mama. Mama baking bread, reading Ben a story, helping her with her English composition, walking out the front door with Ellen to wrap bandages for the war. Mama was strict and demanding, but she was also kind and loved her family whole-heartedly. Alice was so glad *her* mama was just going downtown, coming back in several days, and not gone forever in a grave like so many other mothers these hard days.

Scooping Caleb into her arms, Alice gave him a tight hug. He wouldn't have to lose his mama to a dark hole either. Mrs. Longwell got stronger each day and Anna was on the mend, too.

After washing the dinner dishes, rocking Caleb to sleep, and checking on Mrs. Longwell and Anna, Alice's body was exhausted, but her mind wouldn't rest. Instead of going into the softly lit parlor to read with her family, Alice turned toward her tree. Maybe Alex had left a note for her in the crevice. The black branches jutted out against the paler night sky. Grabbing a rough limb in both hands, she walked her feet up the sturdy trunk. Unladylike, she wrapped her legs around a bough and pulled herself into her thinning leafy haven. She stuffed her hated mask into her pocket.

Eyes stared at her from a nearby perch. Her heart leapt from her chest and she caught a small branch, preventing herself from tumbling out of the tree. She looked again through the shadowy darkness. Yes, eyes. Human eyes.

"Alice." Her name drifted softly through the branches like a falling leaf.

"Alex?" Alice asked, but she knew it was him.

He moved toward the center branches, closer. Alice scooted toward him.

"I hoped you would come," he said. His voice was rough, like he'd been crying. His hands wrung a piece of white cloth. His mask.

Concerned, she asked, "What are you doing out here this late?"

"We got a telegram."

Alice remained quiet, afraid to hear the news. The silence was alive between them, filled with unspoken questions and answers. Finally Alex broke it.

"Father's been injured. It didn't say how bad. He's coming home."

"Oh, Alex," Alice cried giving him a hug. Her relief that Alex's father was alive and coming home was quickly replaced by fear about the seriousness of his injuries. "When will he be home?"

"In a week or two."

More silence. Alice watched patches of moonlight dance across the branches.

"I'm glad he's coming home," Alex said. "Sometimes I look at his photograph and can't remember him any other way—like all he's done all his life is stand around in his best suit with his elbow leaning on a pillar and his right hand in his pocket." He paused. "I mean, I know he worked long hours at the store and helped me with my school work and read the paper and smoked his pipe. I just can't see him doing those things anymore. It's like my memory's foggy."

"He's been gone a long time."

"Too long. I can't wait for him to come home so we can do something fun and normal." He sat quietly a moment. "I want to discuss books with him, play ball in the backyard. I want to build a carousel with him with the new pieces of my erector set." Alex's voice trailed off. "If he's up to it."

"He'll probably be fine. He could help build an erector set carousel. It just may be awhile until he can ride the Coney Island carousel."

"That's another thing I'd like to do. Go to Coney Island again."

They hadn't been there for two years, since the war had disrupted their lives.

"To ride Dip the Dips?" Alice asked.

"You know I hate roller coasters."

"Well you're in luck," Alice said. "They took it down this summer."

"And built a new one called the same thing."

"Hmmm." Alice pretended to search her mind. "I seem to recall that now," she teased. "We'll have to try the new one next summer."

"I'd rather ride the carousel."

"The animals are beautiful. My favorite's still the tiger—all those stripes. What's yours?"

Alex thought a moment. "Whatever's next to the tiger. I like to ride with you."

The laughter and teasing flew into the night like a startled bird.

"I like to ride with you, too," Alice said softly. Her heart fluttered.

"Alice?"

"Yes?" Butterflies darted around her insides.

"May I kiss you? I mean if you want to…if you think it would be all right…"

Alice stopped his stumbling with one word. "Yes."

The night air tasted fresh and cool, like damp earth. Leaves fluttered softly around them. Moonlight patched Alex's hair, cheeks, lips.

Alice turned her face up toward his and their lips met. Soft lips. Clumsy lips, but nice. Alice's dreams of the past few months had come true. Her heart filled with happiness.

# Chapter Nineteen

The morning sun formed yellow squares on the hardwood floor as Alice danced around the parlor bouncing Caleb on her hip and singing.

> K-K-K-Katy, beautiful Katy,
> You're the only g-g-g-girl that I adore;
> When the m-m-m-moon shines,
> Over the cowshed,
> I'll be waiting at the k-k-k-kitchen door.

She tweaked Caleb's nose between her fingers.
"No Katy," he protested. "My Caleb."
"I know you are sweetie. Let me see…"

> C-C-C-Caleb, beautiful Caleb,
> You're the only b-b-b-boy that I adore;
> When the m-m-m-moon shines,
> Over the cowshed,
> I'll be waiting at the k-k-k-kitchen door.

Caleb laughed and clapped his hands. "Again. Again."
Alice sang the song three more times as she twirled the boy around the room, then collapsed exhausted to the floor.
"Again! Again."
"You wore me out, Caleb. Maybe later."
"Pony wide!"
"I'm sure Alex the pony will be by later to give you a ride. He's probably helping his mama at the store." That's where he'd been all

yesterday.

Alice had missed Alex every minute Friday. Because he had been gone so long helping her with Grandpa Thursday, there was extra work to catch up on. Plus, Mr. Wenner had still not recovered enough to come back to work.

Caleb said, "Mama."

"Would you like to visit your mama?" Alice asked, the idea popping into her head and onto her lips at the same time. Mrs. Longwell was looking better every day. She was still weak, but maybe seeing Caleb would help her feel better. She hadn't seen her son in over two weeks.

"Yeah!" Caleb squealed and clapped.

He tried to pull Alice to her feet with his pudgy arms. She got up, called to Ellen and Ben who were making beds upstairs, and the two headed across the grass and fallen leaves between their houses.

Mrs. Longwell was thrilled to see her son. Caleb practically knocked his mother over, leaping into her arms. In the bedroom Alice tended to Anna and read her a story while mother and son visited in the parlor. The children stayed separated. Alice couldn't face Caleb getting sick just because she had brought him home.

In the afternoon as Caleb napped, Alice snuck up to her room to write to Paul. She was supposed to be ironing sheets, a job she hated because of its tedium and uselessness. Who saw if sheets were wrinkled anyway? A few lumps couldn't hurt.

She inked her pen and began.

*Saturday, October 26, 1918*

*Dear Paul,*
 *Thank you for your last letter. I'm glad to hear you're working so hard. I didn't know you knew how to work. Ha ha. Like you, I have been very busy...*

Alice dipped and wrote, dipped and wrote, pouring her thoughts, feelings, and activities onto page after page. Time faded away.

> *You won't believe my news about Alex...*

"Alice." Alice jumped, dragging the 'x' in Alex halfway across the paper. Turning, she found Ellen, hands on hips, standing in the doorway. She looked just like Mama when she was angry.
"Almost finished," Alice said.
"You mean you *are* finished. I went out to weed the garden over an hour ago and left you with the sheets. I come inside and find the sheets still piled in the basket, wrinkled as a handkerchief stuffed in a pocket."
"One more sentence and I'll be done," Alice said. "I'm writing to Paul. He needs to know what goes on at home."
Ellen's angry grimace softened a little. "Finish up quick. Paul needs letters, but Father needs ironed sheets, too."
"Be right down." Alice returned to her writing.
Ellen's footsteps faded then grew louder again. "Alice?"
Alice turned around, not startled this time by Ellen's quiet voice. "Say hello to Paul for me, please."
"I'll write it now," Alice said, and smiled.
"I haven't written him as often as I should. The housework is so hard to stay on top of. If I stop a minute I'm sure the house will fall apart. But I've been meaning to write to Paul more often."
"I'll let him know. And I'll be down to iron the sheets in a jiffy."
"Thank you, Alice." Ellen left for the second time.

> *Ellen sends a 'hello' and an apology for not writing more often. She working like a postman at Christmas. She really is. I've got to go help out now. Ironing sheets! Ugh.*
>       *Your (favorite) sister,*
>       *Allie*
> *P.S. About Alex—he kissed me!!!!*

Alice hummed "K-K-K-Katy" as she addressed the envelope. Ellen had been almost nice. Even thanked her. She could be a good sister sometimes, when she wasn't so concerned about being perfect. Alice danced through the bedroom and out the door.

After dinner, Father waited as Ellen placed a warm apple pie in a basket for him to take to the Schultzes. Mr. Schultz worked with Father and his wife had fallen ill.

"Mmmm. My favorite. Good thing you girls made two or the Schultzes would be doing without."

Alice turned from washing the dishes. "You really would have kept the pie for yourself and left Mr. Schultz and his children without?" she asked, knowing Father was kidding.

"I guess I could have spared a slice or two. I just really miss apple pie. It's not autumn without it. And with most of the sugar going to the war effort, this is probably the only pie I'll get this fall." He rubbed his full stomach.

Ellen peeked in the sugar tin. "You're probably right. Almost empty."

"Be back soon," Father said as he took the basket and headed out the door.

Alice called after him, "Tell Mrs. Schultz we hope she gets better soon."

"I'll give *Mr.* Schultz the message. I'm not traipsing into an influenza sick room."

Soon after Father left, the dinner dishes were dried and stacked neatly in the cupboard and Caleb was curled around his teddy bear deep in sleep. Ben built a Lincoln Log cabin and Ellen stitched on a sampler she was sewing for her hope chest, while Alice slipped out to her tree.

Alice had never seen much use in a hope chest. Why spend hours sewing pillow cases and doilies when you could be climbing trees or visiting with friends? Now she thought maybe she'd start one. Alex might like nice things in their house some day. She blushed at the thought as she strode through the back yard.

Alex hadn't appeared all day, so maybe he was in the tree branches waiting for her like he was two nights ago. Or maybe he at the least left a note.

"Alex?" she called softly.

No answer. He'd better not be hiding up there. She hoisted herself cautiously onto the lowest limb, bracing herself for a surprise attack. Persistent leaves fluttered on emptying branches in the setting sunlight. Where could he be? She slid her hand into their mail crevice, hoping for news. Pain shot up her arm and she yanked her hand out like pulling it from a lion's jaws. An inch long splinter jutted from under her fingernail.

"Ow!" she protested to the tree. As her finger throbbed, she plucked at the giant sliver with her good hand, working it out from under the nail.

She slid her mask off her face to pop her injured finger into her mouth. It still hurt.

Gingerly, Alice swung out of the tree. She knelt and plunged her hand into the icy creek. Her hand turned prickly with the cold, dulling the pain. When the frigid water became unbearable, Alice pulled her hand out and wrapped it in her dress skirt.

The sun dipped lower and lower in the sky, painting the clouds orange and pink. Minutes ticked by as Alice sat by the frolicking creek, nursing her bleeding finger. Still no Alex. Worry, then dread filled Alice's heart. Something had to be wrong.

Maybe he was embarrassed by their kiss. Did he still want to be around her? Was their friendship ruined? The questions filled her mind and she had to find answers.

Ignoring her throbbing finger, she stood. Leaves crunched under her shoes as she walked briskly toward Alex's house. She decided Mrs. Beck would prefer she use the front door instead of the trellis, so she climbed the porch steps and knocked. No answer.

That was odd. She knocked again. Could they already be in bed? The sun wasn't even down yet. Were they still at the store?

Alice went around the side of the house and called, "Alex?" Faint light glowed in his open bedroom window.

Carefully in the fading daylight, Alice placed hands and feet on the trellis and climbed. As her eyes cleared the window sill, she stared hard into the dim room. A lumpy shape filled Alex's bed. Alice pried open the window and scrambled over the sill. She landed in a heap on several bars of Alex's erector set which were scattered on the wooden floor. The clang of metal on metal pierced the night as the pieces skittered across the floor. The lump in the bed didn't move.

Picking herself up, she darted on tip-toe to the bedside. Alex's curly dark locks lay on the white pillow and his pain-filled, glassy eyes stared into her shocked ones.

"Alex!" She sat on the bed and took his limp hand. It was on fire. His face looked bluish green in the lamplight and his breaths came in gasps. A sudden fit of coughing violently shook his body. He covered his mouth with a cloth clutched in his other hand. When the coughing finally stopped, Alex dropped his hand back to his side, exhausted. The cloth was covered in bright red blood.

"Alice! What are you doing here?" Alice jumped at Mrs. Beck's frantic voice. She stood at the door holding a small bowl.

"I came to see Alex."

"You must leave, dear. It's the influenza."

"I can't leave, Mrs. Beck. I have to be with him."

"At least put your mask on, child." Alice tied the mask. She stared into Mrs. Beck's frightened eyes, sure her own eyes mirrored the terror. "He took sick this morning. I sent him to stack potatoes sacks and found him collapsed on the floor."

"But he was fine."

"I know, I know." Mrs. Beck dropped into a chair next to the bed. The bowl filled with a dark liquid rested in her lap. She painstakingly poured spoonful after spoonful of the drink between Alex's blue lips. The liquid smelled horrible, like terpentine, but Alex didn't resist.

Alice noticed a ring of chicken feathers encircling Alex's neck. Mrs. Beck must be trying every cure she'd heard of to keep Alex alive. Something had to work.

"Water," Alex gasped.

Alice took a glass from the night table and held it to his lips. Rivulets ran down his chin, dampening the feathers, but most of the water went down.

"You really should leave, Alice," Mrs. Beck insisted.

"Just let me stay a little while. I can take care of him. I've been helping with the Longwells. Maybe you could rest. It will probably be a long night."

Worry blanketed Mrs. Beck's features. She looked years older than she had yesterday. Swiping at a bleary eye, she said, "You may stay one hour. Promise you'll wake me."

"I will, Mrs. Beck. Thank you."

Mrs. Beck slipped out of the room. The room was silent but for Alex's groans and raspy breaths. His eyes were closed, tightly. Alice held his hand and watched the lamplight dance across his troubled face. She prayed that he would get well.

He opened his eyes and looked directly into hers. Between gasps he muttered, "Alice."

"Don't try to talk. I'm here. Your mama and I will take care of you. You'll see. Everything will be fine. In no time you'll be giving Caleb pony rides and sitting in my tree." Alice rambled on, not sure which of them she was trying to convince.

"I...don't...think...I'll get...better. I feel...so...bad."

"You have to get better, Alex. Your father's coming home. He can't wait to see you. You'll build that carousel together."

Coughing wracked Alex's body again. As the coughing slowed, he pulled the rag away from his mouth. Blood covered his chin and ran out his nose. Alice grabbed a new cloth from a pile on the dresser and sopped up the blood. The blood she wiped away was immediately replaced by new rivers of red, flowing down his cheeks toward each ear. She pinched his nose, trying to stop the bleeding. Over her hands, Alex's eyes studied her face, as if memorizing her features.

Eventually, the nose bleed slowed to a trickle, then stopped. Alice piled the scarlet soaked rags on a corner of the bed and went to the wash stand against the wall. She slipped her hands into the cool, clear water, turning it a marbled pink. She dried her hands on a towel hanging next to the basin and returned to Alex.

He was still watching her, tracking her movements across the room. "Alice."

"Yes, Alex?"

"Promise me something." He squeezed his eyes shut and grabbed his head in both hands.

"Does your head hurt?" Alice asked.

"Doesn't...matter," he said through clenched teeth. "Promise."

"What do you want me to promise?"

"Promise you'll be...happy."

"I am happy with you, Alex. I've never been happier in my life."

"No...promise you'll be happy...without me."

Tears filled Alice's eyes. "I can't promise that, Alex. I don't have to promise that. You'll be fine. You'll see. Mrs. Longwell's getting better and so is Anna. You will, too."

"Promise," Alex said a little louder.

Alice looked through tears into Alex's pain filled eyes for a long moment. "I promise," she whispered.

His eyes seemed to relax slightly.

"Alice."

"Yes?" Alice's voice cracked. Sobs shook her body as she held both of Alex's hands with all her might.

"I love you."

"I love you, too, Alex." Alice collapsed onto his chest. Her tears formed warm puddles on the quilt under her cheeks.

# Chapter Twenty

Alice awoke to golden sunshine streaming through her window and dark memories streaming through her mind. How could the day be sunny? Alex had the influenza.

She jumped out of bed, dressed, scrubbed her face in the wash basin, and flew down the stairs.

As she darted through the parlor to the front door, a soft voice called, "Alice."

Alice spun around and discovered Father sitting statue-like in his tall armchair in the corner, Bible in hand.

"Father, you startled me!"

"Come here, Alice." He patted his knee. She crossed the room to climb into his lap like she had as a little girl. She felt his strong arms encircle her. "On your way to see Alex?"

"Yes."

"This influenza's an awful disease. I've worried and prayed about Alex since you came home with the news last night."

"I need to go to him."

"I'll let you go. However, you can't spend every waking hour with Alex."

"But, Father..."

"He's very sick and I don't want you falling ill. You've taken so many chances already caring for the sick. I'll allow you to help care for Alex, but have some breakfast first. Say a prayer for Alex at our family church service. Then go to him."

"Yes, sir," Alice said dejectedly. She wanted to go now.

Father squeezed her tight and she returned his hug, then slid off his lap.

"Help your sister get breakfast on. She's making extra for the Schultzes. Now me, I could live on apple pie alone, but Ellen insists they need more nourishment. I'm sure she's making up a basket for the Becks too. You can take it over after services."

"I will, Father," Alice said on her way to the kitchen.

The kitchen clanks and clatters seemed abnormally loud. The everyday chatter and laughter were missing. The bacon sizzled and popped in Mama's black skillet as Ellen silently turned the slices with a fork. Ben sat at the table, a pencil motionless in his hand, staring out the window. Even Caleb was momentarily quiet as he concentrated on twisting and tugging the white buttons on his shirt.

Three pairs of eyes turned to Alice. Ellen set down the fork and gave Alice a hug.

"I'm sorry about Alex," she whispered in Alice's hair.

Alice felt tears coming again. She dabbed at the corners of her eyes with her fingers. Ellen released her and Ben gave her a hug, burying his head in her dress. "Is Alex going to be okay?" he asked.

"I hope so, Ben. I'll take good care of him."

At hearing Alex's name a smile covered Caleb's face. "Pony wide, pony wide!" he shouted, pounding the table with his hands.

Alice put her hands on Caleb's shoulders. "I hope Alex will be over soon to give you a pony ride," she said. The child's hair became a muddled pool the color of corn stalks as Alice's tears flowed. She sat next to Caleb to collect herself.

Once breakfast was over and the dishes washed, Ellen and Alice made up baskets for the Becks and the Schultzes. They joined Father and the boys in the parlor for an informal church service. Caleb made it more casual than usual by clapping and "singing" his own version of each hymn Ellen selected. Ellen played the piano in Mama's absence. The prayers were the longest part of the service. Alice thought they could have prayed all day and not have had time to pray for each person that needed praying for. She prayed hardest for Alex.

At Father's last "amen" Alice hurried to the kitchen to collect the basket of food. Ellen followed her into the kitchen.

Picking up father's basket Ellen said, "Don't be gone too long."

"I won't. I'll come home in an hour or two, then go back again later. That way Mrs. Beck can rest. She's probably had a long night. I wish Mama were here so I could ask her what she put in the Longwells' medicine. I could bring some to Alex."

"I don't know if the medicine helped any, but I know most of the ingredients she used. I'll make some for you to take over this afternoon."

"Thank you, Ellen." She gave Ellen a quick hug, then headed out the back door.

The air had turned crisp overnight and Alice shivered. She returned to the Becks' front door, because climbing the trellis was hard enough without carrying a basket.

She rounded the side of Alex's house, listing in her mind the things she would talk to him about today—his father coming home soon, school starting again, Caleb wanting a pony "wide." She wanted to distract him from the pain—help him feel better. She climbed the porch steps. White crepe paper fluttered past her eyes. A party? While Alex was sick?

No. White crepe paper.

The world went black.

# Chapter Twenty-one

"Alice. Alice, are you awake?" Alice heard Ellen's words, but didn't move. Her eyes stared blankly at her bedroom wall and a sunny window corner. A chill ran through her rag-doll arms which draped loosely at her sides and her legs ached to be stretched. She didn't shift her position one inch. Maybe if she lay in bed long enough, she'd die. Die like Alex.

Ellen's dark blurred form moved across the patch of window light. "Alice. I brought you some biscuits and jam."

Alice felt the heaviness of the bed quilt placed over her. The shivers stopped. She remained still, staring.

"Alice, I'll leave this tray for you. I'll check on you again in a while. Try to eat something."

The door clicked closed. Dust motes danced in the streaming sunbeams, but Alice remained motionless.

The window darkened in one corner as a head rose over the sill, followed by broad shoulders and long arms and legs. The figure climbed through the window. He was dressed in olive green. A soldier? Why was a soldier climbing in her bedroom window?

"Hi ya, Allie!"

"Paul!" Alice sat up in bed and threw her arms around her big brother. "What are you doing here?"

"They stationed my company here. I'm on the front line."

"The front line? How can you be on the front line in Cincinnati? The Germans aren't here, are they?"

"Not the Germans, the influenza! It's been sneaking into Cincinnati for weeks now, but we'll get it, don't you worry. It's tricky, but we're the best soldiers the U.S. Army has ever seen!"

"You're too late! The influenza has already killed Alex."

Paul touched Alice's shoulder, comfortingly. "I'm sorry, Allie."

Alice looked down at her lap. She found long bars of an erector set resting in the skirt of her favorite peach dress. Alex's erector set. Absentmindedly she fitted the pieces together, connecting them with screws and washers. She looked up.

Over Paul's shoulder Alice saw a second dark figure clamber in the window. He had tousled dark hair, his wire-rimmed glasses were askew, and he was moving fast.

"Help me, Alice!"

"Alex?"

"Help!"came the terrified reply.

Alex darted around the bed and crouched in the corner.

Alice turned to the window to figure out what Alex was so afraid of.

An ink-black little bird with blood-red eyes swooped in the window screaching, "Enza! Enza! Enza!" It darted at Alex and began furiously pecking at his head and beating his face with its wings. Alex covered his eyes and head as best he could. Suddenly, the bird stopped its attack, and flew to the dresser top. From its high perch it glared down at Alice with its beady red eyes and in a scratchy, squawk began chanting:

You *had a little bird*
*Her name was Enza*
You *opened the window*
*And in-flu-Enza!*

The bird shrieked a hideous laugh.

Alice cried, "I didn't open the window! I didn't mean to! I didn't mean it!"

She turned to Paul who was now standing by the open window. A strong wind whipped the curtains and the sky had turned to night.

"Paul, tell it I didn't mean to let influenza in! Tell it to go away and leave Alex alone!"

Paul smiled. "Gotta go, Allie. They need me to fight. Besides, I just heard the mess hall bell. They're serving up meatloaf tonight! You know how I love meatloaf!" Paul disappeared into the night.

"Don't go, Paul! I need you!" Alice screamed.

She turned back to the bird who was eyeing Alex again. Alice grabbed an erector set bar and ran at the bird. It flew into the air, darting around the room, diving at Alex every chance it got. Alice swung at it over and over as it swooped over her head.

Finally it perched on the dresser again, a satisfied, smug look on its face as it stared at Alex. Alice stopped, chest pounding, and turned to Alex. He lay crumpled on the floor, blood trickling from the wounds the bird's beak had made.

"Alice." She could barely hear his weak voice. "I can't fight it. I'm sorry. I tried."

He looked sorrowfully at Alice, then closed his eyes.

"No!" Alice screamed.

The evil bird's squawked words filled the room, her mind:

<blockquote>
You opened the window<br>
And in-flu-Enza!<br>
You opened the window<br>
And in-flu-Enza!
</blockquote>

"No! I didn't mean to! Alex, come back!"

The bird swooped at Alice, slashing at her with its razor-sharp wings and beak.

"Noooo!" Alice shrieked.

"Alice!"

"Noooo! Get away from me! Give Alex back!"

"Alice! Wake up!"

Alice stopped struggling and opened her eyes. The bird disappeared. Ellen's frightened face appeared inches from her own as she shook Alice awake.

"Ellen?"

"Yes," Ellen said, relief in her voice.

Moving only her head, Alice glanced around the room. The evil bird was truly gone, as was Alex's body. Night had returned to day.

"Alex! Where's Alex?"

Ellen squeezed Alice's shoulders. "His funeral was this morning. Only his mama and Pastor Grady were allowed to go." Alice stared at the ceiling, trying to untangle her dreamed nightmare from her real nightmare.

"I was having a bad dream."

Ellen nodded.

"An evil black bird attacked and killed Alex. It was Influenza. Actually it was Enza and it kept repeating that I had let it in. I tried to fight it, but I couldn't."

"Oh, Alice!"

Alice was silent a moment. Finally she asked, "Do you think it was right?"

"What?"

"The creature. Do you think I made Alex get sick?"

"Of course not," Ellen said quickly.

"It was my idea to take a walk on the day we found Miss Lang. And he took care of Anna for me. He could have gotten sick from someone on the trolley when we visited Grandpa."

"Alex could have caught the influenza anywhere. He worked in the store. Wasn't Mr. Wenner, their worker, sick? And Alex ran errands for his mama. Who knows why he got so sick so fast? No one even knows for sure how people catch the flu."

Alice worked to believe Ellen, but she wasn't convinced.

"Alice, you cannot blame yourself for Alex dying. It wasn't your fault."

"Remember? You told me I was bringing the flu home to the family."

"Yes, but you didn't bring it home. And you didn't bring it to Alex." Ellen's voice wavered. Her eyes brimmed with tears. "You had to help those sick people. That's you and Alex loved that in you. He wouldn't have wanted you to be any different. You care so much, Alice."

Alice turned away as fresh tears poured down her cheeks. "I loved him, Ellen."

Ellen took her hand and squeezed. "I see that. And I'm sure he loved you."

"He told me he did—the night he died."

"I could see it in him. His face lit up whenever he was around you. He loved how you enjoy life and how much you care about people."

Alice's tears flowed into her faint smile as she remembered their fun at the zoo, racing through the streets of Cincinnati, visiting Grandpa, romping with the children, talking in her tree, the kiss.

The kiss! Her smile faded as a new fear gripped her heart. She and Alex had kissed—without masks—just before he got sick! Maybe she would be bringing the flu home to the family after all.

# Chapter Twenty-two

Alice pushed the quilt off her legs and swung her feet to the floor. By November, getting out of bed would send chills down her spine as the ice cold air attacked her cozy body. But the end of October was not uncomfortably chilly. She looked over her shoulder at the other side of the bed. The quilt's colorful patches marched up and over Ellen's still form. Alice would be extra quiet so Ellen could sleep.

She padded barefoot across the floor and sat down at the little table by the window. Rain slid down the window panes and bounced off the red and yellow painted leaves in the yard.

Mama should come home today. She had only been gone a little more than three days, and yet it seemed like three months to Alice. Her life had changed—forever. Father had offered to bring Mama home last night, but Alice had refused. Grandpa needed Mama the most right now.

Alice had longed for a telephone, so that she could at least hear Mama's comforting voice. But they didn't have one and Grandpa didn't have a telephone to receive the call anyway. Grandpa "wouldn't have one of those contraptions clanging away at him every minute of the day as he tried to eat his supper or read the paper." The only chance she had of talking to Mama was to sit at the Becks' store all day and wait for a call and she couldn't bare to do that.

Alice had spent Sunday evening doing everyday things, trying to make her life go back to normal; trying to keep Alex alive. But her tears welled up until she couldn't see the spot she was scrubbing on the kitchen floor. Dark saltwater patches spotted the sheets she ironed. Tears plopped softly into the dish water.

While Father kept Ben occupied in the parlor, Ellen followed Alice from chore to chore, a quiet, comforting presence all evening. She helped scrub the floor and folded the salt-watered sheets Alice ironed.

As Alice handed Ellen a dripping dish to dry she heard a soft rap on the kitchen door. Her heart leaped! Alex! She raced to the door and flung it open. Mr. Schultz's startled face stared back at her, Mama's empty pie plate in his hand. Alice, equally stunned, dropped the dish, smashing it to bits on the well-scrubbed wooden floor. She fled the kitchen, flew up the stairs, and buried her head in her pillow.

Ellen soon followed. Alice felt her weight as she sat on the bed, heard her quiet "there, there"'s as she softly rubbed Alice's back. The tears flowed and flowed until Alice thought she could build a boat and sail away on them; a salt-water river of sadness.

And still Ellen sat with her.

The hypnotizing raindrops continued to roll down the bedroom window as Alice stared and remembered. Ellen was a good sister. Alice shook her head to clear her mind of rain and memories and slid a clean sheet of paper out of the table drawer. It had been Ellen's idea to do what Alice was about to do—say good-bye to Alex. She dipped her pen into the ink well and began.

*Wednesday October 30, 1918*

*My dearest Alex,*
   *I probably never would have called you "dearest" in life—too sappy or adult or something—but now that you're gone, I will. It fits. You were my best friend and you gave me my first kiss. Maybe it will be my only kiss. It will be hard to find someone I care for as much as you. I have a giant hole in my heart now that you are gone. I wish you could have gotten better, but I know you must have tried your best. I'm sorry if you got sick because of me. Ellen tells me you wouldn't want me to blame myself, so I will try not to. Always remember me. I will always remember you. I will try to keep my promise to you, but right now, I cannot be happy. Good-bye.*
                                                                                    *Your Alice*

Alice read the letter through and blew on the ink to help it dry. A tear tumbled off her cheek smearing the 'ce' in Alice. She blew harder to dry the salty ink puddle.

Leaving the letter on the table, Alice stood to dress. The steel blue material of Alice's plainest dress swished quietly over her head. Alice had often protested wearing the scratchy, unadorned frock. Now, as she struggled to slide her arms through the prickly sleeves she was glad to have it. It fit her feelings perfectly. She ran a brush through her hair and omitted the ribbon. On tiptoe, Alice collected her letter from the table and shoes from the floor, and slipped noiselessly out the door.

Ben's quiet snores filled the hallway as she crept down the stairs. In the kitchen, instead of finding Father rereading the paper from the night before, she found a small, white note on the table:

> *Girls,*
> *Went in early to help with the extra work at the post office. Don't worry about breakfast as I brought along some biscuits. Growing, hardworking girls need their sleep.*
> *Father*

Alice left her shoes at the kitchen door, folded her letter to Alex into her pocket, and went outside. The rain-soaked grass was slippery and cold on her bare toes as she walked toward her tree. Pulling herself into the maple's dripping branches her foot slipped on the wet bark and she hit her knee hard on the trunk. Pain shot through her leg and she cried out. She stopped momentarily to examine the scrape. Blood mixed with rain, trickled down her calf and disappeared in the grass. She grasped the limbs a second time and hoisted herself into the tree. The thick, green canopy of leaves, which had protected her from the sun's rays through the summer, had turned a patchy, brilliant red.

She wanted to be with Alex, wanted him to tug on her foot from the base of the tree and tell her it had all been a bad dream. She glanced down at the ground beneath—hoping. No Alex, just rain-soaked grass and browning scarlet leaves.

Out of habit, she checked the crevice. Something smooth and thin like paper brushed her fingertips. She yanked her hand out, startled. The crevice mail was a secret between Alex and her. Who could have put a letter inside? Carefully she reached back into the hole and pulled out a folded paper. Opening it with shaky fingers, she instantly recognized Alex's small neat handwriting. Her heart jumped.

> Dear Alice,
> *I will remember last night always. I don't know when my feelings for you changed from friendship to more. I am relieved that your feelings have changed toward me also. I can't wait to see you again. Tonight? I can't wait to see Father again, too. He should be home any day now. Our family will be whole again. I'm so happy.*
>
> All my love,
> Alex

Tears poured down Alice's cheeks as she read the letter again and again, shielding the precious words from the rain with her hand. Alex must have written it the day before he died. He had been so happy. They both had been. She wrapped her goose-bumped arms around her drawn-up knees and read once again.

The drizzly rain mingled with the warm tears on Alice's cheeks. It formed an intricate pattern of lacy dark patches on her simple dress and collected in rivulets which rolled down her hair and neck as she cried. Could a person cry herself to death?

Eventually her tears and the rain slowed. She slipped Alex's last letter to her into her pocket and pulled out her final letter to him. Her folded body had prevented the black ink from mingling with the rain and destroying her words. She read her thoughts and feelings out loud—to Alex—and knew he heard her even if he couldn't be there to comfort her. She just knew. Folding the letter carefully before it got too damp, she stuffed it into the crevice.

Alice felt worn out, exhausted from her sadness. She swung out of the tree and headed back toward the house, making footprint impressions in the damp grass. Inside, the house was quiet and still. The mantle clock's ornate hands pointed to the ten and the twelve as it ticked out the seconds in the shadowy parlor. Ten o'clock. Ellen sure was sleeping a long time.

A giggle danced down the stairs. Ben. Alice climbed the steps and found her brother sitting on his bed, looking at the green *Aesop's Fables* book with the lion on the cover.

"What's so funny?" Alice asked, leaning against the door frame.

"The man and the boy carrying the donkey!" Ben laughed again and Alice smiled.

She knew the story well about the father, the son, and the donkey. As the three went to market people complained that the boy was lazy for letting his father walk while he rode. So they switched places. Then people complained that the man let his little son walk while he rode. So they both rode and people complained that they were being mean to the donkey. Finally, they ended up carrying the donkey. It was a pretty funny story that taught that you shouldn't try to please everyone.

Feeling slightly better for smiling, Alice stepped into the room and patted Ben's slicked-down hair. He must have wetted it down and combed it before climbing back into bed to read. She smiled again at her odd little brother. Maybe some day her hurt would go away and she'd be able to laugh again. For now she'd have to be satisfied with an occasional grin.

A low moan drifted into the room and stabbed Alice in the heart. The smile left. Another groan followed. Alice yanked Ben onto his feet and they raced across the hall.

# Chapter Twenty-three

After letting go of Ben's hand, Alice pulled the covers from Ellen's chin. Ellen's terrified, pain-filled eyes stared over her double mask. The masks were flecked with bright red splotches and her face had a bluish cast. Her honey hair twisted in snakelike tangled coils around her face, spilling onto the white pillow. Alice smoothed back one unruly lock and felt her sister's forehead. Scalding hot. Ellen's moan shot up Alice's spine.

Alice looked away. Not again. Ben sat at the edge of the room, arms and legs wrapped protectively around his little body, rocking back and forth. Mama may not be home for hours. Father had left for work.

"Help me, Alice." Ellen's voice was raspy and her breaths shallow.

Alice forced herself to look straight into Ellen's feverish eyes. 'I can't' flashed through her mind. The sickness is too strong. But she heard her voice reassuring Ellen. "I'll take care of you. Don't worry."

She pulled the quilt back up to Ellen's hot chin, then darted past Ben into the dim hall. She leaned hard against the wall, and slid to the floor, covering her face with her hands.

Thoughts and emotions whirled through Alice's head like a tornado. She would give anything to go back in time a few weeks or even a few days to be out of this nightmare. She'd even be happy to be back moments ago, in Ben's room, smiling about people carrying a donkey. A spider crawled across the floor by her big toe and folded itself into a crevice in the floor. Oh, to join that spider—to disappear into an influenza-free world. The spider didn't have to worry about its family members suddenly getting sick.

Just squished. The odd thought popped unbidden into her swirl of frustrated, frightened thoughts. In a way they were all like spiders—fine one day—squished the next. Alex, then Ellen. Who would be next? Ben? Alice? Alice couldn't let this heartless disease win. She'd fight to the death. It had taken Alex. It would not take her family one by one, not if she could help it.

She jumped to her feet, nearly tripping over Ben, who had crouched at her side without her noticing. Sniffling, he looked up at her with wide, frightened eyes. He had his thumb in his mouth, a habit given up years ago.

Alice pulled him to his feet by his thumb-sucking arm, popping the offending finger out of his mouth with a loud thwack. She stood her brother at arm's length and looked into his saucer eyes. "Everything will be okay, Ben. You'll see." She tried to reassure both of them.

"I want Mama!" Ben whimpered.

"I do too, Ben." *You don't know how much*, she added to herself. "But she won't be home for awhile. For now, it's you and me. Can I count on you? Can Ellen?"

Ben straightened to his full six-year-old height, arms straight at his sides. He wiped his gooey thumb off on his white night shirt. "You can count on me, Alice," he said like a little soldier.

"Good." She squeezed his shoulder. "Now go get dressed while I think."


Alice didn't waste a minute. By the time Ben was dressed, neat as a pin and shoes crisply tied, Alice had straightened out Ellen's sheets, applied a cold cloth to her head, and was in the parlor, searching through a pile of old newspapers for influenza remedies. Father had chuckled at some of the far-fetched ideas as he read the paper to the family each night. "Turpentine and sugar, malted milk? Those are more likely to kill you or make you fat than cure you."

But, Alice was desperate. She didn't know Mama's ingredients for the Longwells' medicine, only Ellen did. Alice had questioned Ellen as she tried to make her more comfortable. Did she use onions? Red peppers? Kerosene? She was nearly certain about the kerosene. But how much? Ellen mumbled "unyans," then closed her eyes. What else? No medicine had only one ingredient.

Mrs. Beck's turpentine remedy hadn't helped Alex, but he had fallen sick so quickly, probably nothing would have helped. Alice had to do something. Doing something, anything, was better than sitting idly by as the influenza killed Ellen.

Flipping through a week-old paper, Alice came across an advertisement by a Dr. Walters. He claimed to be with dozens of flu patients each day and said he never got sick because he drank ordinary baking soda in water. It couldn't stop Ellen from getting sick, but maybe it could stop her from getting sicker.

"Ben," Alice called to her brother who was rocking frantically in Mama's rocking chair. "Go to the kitchen and fetch a glass of water and the baking soda. Baking *soda*, not powder." She paused. "Better make it three glasses of water. Then wait for me."

Alice searched through the newspapers again, like a squirrel frantically digging for buried nuts. Her finger zig-zagged quickly from top to bottom of each page. *Influenza, Epidemic,* and *Flu* jumped out at her in bold, black type.

One author recommended onions. Another swore by goose-grease poultices, cloths soaked in goose-grease. Yuck. Kerosene and turpentine were mentioned.

She looked up from her search. Where else had she heard ideas to stop the flu? Odd phrases popped into her mind. Chew food carefully. Wash hands often. Get fresh air. Miss Lang!

Miss Lang's pamphlet had mentioned several common sense ideas. Miss Lang herself had talked about little bags of garlic gum. That might work. Garlic cloves hung drying in the pantry, waiting to spice soups and roasts this winter. Maybe Alice would use them for something more important: curing Ellen.

Chicken feathers. Mrs. Lang had mentioned them too. She'd pluck every chicken in Cincinnati bald if it would save Ellen, but she doubted they'd do much. They hadn't helped Alex. A pang gripped her heart. Oh, Alex. Alice saw the limp chicken feathers draping Alex's gasping chest. She blinked the awful picture away and stood.

Alice left the papers in a confused fan across the parlor floor and joined Ben in the kitchen. He was standing on a chair at the sink, filling a third brimming glass of water. Alice took the glass from Ben, poured some of the water back into the sink to make room, and dumped one heaping spoonful of baking soda into each glass. It sunk in white clumps to the bottom. Was one enough? Alice added a little more to each glass, then stirred with a spoon. The lumps dissolved making the water faintly milky.

Ben looked warily at the glasses. "Ellen's gonna drink three glasses?"

"Nope. One for Ellen, one for me, and one for you!"

Ben hopped off the chair and backed away. Alice tried to hand her brother a glass, but he backed into the corner and put his hands over his masked mouth.

"Come on, Ben. Ellen has the influenza. This might stop us from getting it too. We have to try." Removing her mask and pinching her nose, Alice awkwardly gulped down the liquid. Her mouth felt coated by the baking soda. It tasted slightly tangy and salty. Not awful, but definitely not good. She smiled through gritted teeth. "See, I did it." She tried to encourage Ben.

After a few more protests, Ben did the same. He made a face and stuck out his tongue.

"Yuck."

"Here, have some bread to get rid of the taste." Alice sliced a piece for him and another for herself. The baking soda drink and bread reminded Alice's stomach that she hadn't eaten all day. As she chewed her first slice, she cut a second slice for each of them. Swallowing the makeshift meal quickly, they headed upstairs with Ellen's "medicine."

By mid-afternoon, Mama hadn't returned and Ellen's condition hadn't improved. In fact, she seemed worse. Like Alex and little Anna, Ellen would have fits of coughing and then be so still Alice had to check to make sure she was still alive. Blood from Ellen's coughing had seeped through both masks forming a pink and red pattern with very little white. Alice removed the masks, hoping the fresh air would help Ellen breathe better, but Ellen kept feeling her face and tossing to and fro. Finding a clean mask in Ellen's dresser, Alice tied it securely around Ellen's steaming head.

Ben played quietly in his room or sat in the hall talking with Alice as she sat at Ellen's bedside. Alice wanted Ben to stay away from Ellen, lest he get sick, too. At least Caleb was home with his mama and sister now, so she didn't have to worry about him getting too close to Ellen. Mrs. Longwell was weak, but better, and Anna was on the mend too.

Early in the afternoon, Ellen fell into a restless sleep once again.

From her bedside chair, Alice read *Aesop's Fables* to Ben, raising her voice to reach into the hallway.

Around four o'clock Alice's stomach rumbled. She asked Ben to bring apples, bread, and cheese upstairs on a tray. Ben hopped to his feet and dashed down the stairs to help.

Alice was biting into her apple when Ellen started her worst coughing fit yet. The rough coughs shook Ellen's tired, fiery body and blood covered another mask. Gurgling came from her throat and she sounded as if she was choking or drowning. Alice held Ellen up until the coughing stopped, then laid her back down on the pillow.

Ellen looked at Alice with exhausted eyes.

"Don't give up, Ellen," Alice said firmly. "I need you. I love you."

Ellen closed her eyes and fell into a fitful sleep. Alice straightened the quilt, retrieved her apple, and sank hard into the straight-backed wooden chair at Ellen's bedside.

How had this happened? Ellen had been the most careful at avoiding the flu. Maybe it had been on Caleb and Anna's clothes. Or on Alice's clothes for that matter. Maybe Alice spread the disease, but somehow avoided catching it herself. Maybe you caught it from dirt. Ellen did clean a lot. Maybe the masks didn't protect you at all. The unanswerable questions tumbled around her mind.

Tiring of the wondering how, Alice picked up *Aesop's Fables* again. She read story after story aloud to Ben who sprawled with his tin soldiers in the hallway. As the mouse chewed through the net around the captured lion, Ellen screamed.

# Chapter Twenty-four

Startled by Ellen's choked cry, Alice dropped the story book and rushed to her side. She sat down on the bed as Ellen screamed again, the sound garbling up in her congested lungs and throat.

"What's wrong, Ellen?"

Ellen gasped for air between shrieks and pointed toward the window. Alice followed Ellen's shaking finger. For an instant, Alice expected the wicked black bird, Enza, to be perched on the windowsill ready to attack. Nothing was there. The curtains blew softly in the breeze. Ellen covered her face with her hands and kicked out with her legs, one at a time as if she was pedaling a bike. Pressed back against the headboard as far as possible, Ellen peeked between her fingers.

In a surge of energy she pulled herself onto Alice. What was Ellen doing, trying to climb over her? Arms and legs flailed as Alice wrestled to keep Ellen in bed while Ellen frantically worked at escaping. Alice lost her footing and the two tumbled to the floor. Ellen lay still. She seemed exhausted.

But as Alice tried to lift her into bed, Ellen pushed her away and screamed again. Giving up the struggle momentarily, Alice lay Ellen back down on the floor. Ellen's frightened eyes darted wildly around the room. What was she looking at? The side of the bed? The dresser? The doorway where Ben now stood looking almost as scared as Ellen?

"It's all right, Ellen," Alice assured her in a soothing voice. Ellen looked *at* Alice and *through* her at the same time. Did Ellen even see her?

"Ellen, it's me, Alice. Don't be scared."

Alice pulled the cool, damp rag, which had fallen to the floor in the struggle, out from under Ellen's shoulder and placed it back on her forehead. Her head felt even hotter than before. Reaching over Ellen to the bed, Alice managed to pinch a corner of a pillow between outstretched fingers and drag it to the floor. She placed it under Ellen's head. Ellen closed her eyes and fell instantly asleep.

"Ben," Alice whispered. "Go downstairs and get a clove of garlic, a dish towel, and the string Father and Mama use to tie packages. Oh, and scissors. Hurry!"

As Alice watched Ellen for signs of distress, she could hear rapid footsteps, drawers and doors slamming shut, and finally the clatter of Ben hurrying up the stairs. He dropped the requested items at Alice's side.

"Whatcha gonna do?" he asked.

"Miss Lang said tying a bag of garlic around a sick person's neck could help."

Alice broke the clove into pieces and the scent of garlic filled the room and covered her fingers. She wrapped the pieces in the towel, tied the cloth closed, and tied the pungent bundle around Ellen's neck. Ellen didn't stir.

Alice leaned against the chair legs, exhausted herself. Where was Mama? Shouldn't she be home by now? Alice felt her own forehead, checking for fever. A little warm. Maybe she should drink more baking soda water. Too tired to bother, her eyes fluttered closed, then opened, then closed again.

A steady clumping, first faint, then louder, filled her ears. Drums? Knocking? Footsteps? As her foggy mind cleared she opened her eyes to find Father walking into the bedroom.

"Oh, Father," Alice cried. She stood and nearly jumped into his arms. The tears that had been threatening to break loose all afternoon flooded from her eyes. She turned to Ellen who was still asleep, but tossing and turning on the floor, mumbling.

"Ben and I found her sick this morning. It's the influenza. It's bad. Just like Alex was."

Father stooped and felt Ellen's forehead.

Father asked, "Why is she on the floor?"

"I couldn't get her back into bed. She started screaming and acting all crazy. I think she was delirious."

"Her fever must be so high that she's seeing things that aren't really there." He paused and ran his hand through his hair.

He asked, "Where's Ben?"

"Here I am." Ben stood in the doorway, rubbing one eye. He looked like he'd just woken up.

"Come here, son. You, too, Alice." From his kneeling position on the floor, he gathered them in his arms. His cool hand felt Alice's forehead, then Ben's. "Seem normal. That's a blessing. You two have had some day."

"Yes, sir," Alice said, laying her tired head on his warm shoulder.

"I'm going to fetch your mother. I thought she'd be home by now. She'd skin me alive if she knew one of you was sick and I didn't get her. Do you think you can take care of things here?"

Alice looked at Ben and they both nodded.

"I knew I could count on you." He squeezed them in a strong bear hug.

Alice stood and put her arm around Ben's shoulder. Father felt Ellen's cheek, then hovered over her a long moment. Alice thought she could detect his shoulders shaking slightly. Was Father crying?

Finally he gathered Ellen in his arms, stood, and laid her back in bed. He gently adjusted the quilt over her, then quickly left the room. Over his shoulder he called, "Your mama sure will be proud when she hears what a good job you've done." His voice quavered strangely.


Mama was proud. She embraced Alice so hard she thought she might have broken a rib. Alice hugged back. Mama's sweet lilac fragrance mingled with the strong garlic smell in the room.

"I'm so sorry about Alex," Mama whispered into her hair as she smoothed Alice's locks over her head. They squeezed each other even tighter.

With an arm still around Alice, Mama walked over to the bed. Mama checked Ellen precisely the same way Alice had been caring for her all day. She smoothed the quilts and turned to Alice.

"I couldn't have cared for her better myself. Caring for all those sick people prepared you for this. I'm glad you are so dependable, Alice."

Alice smiled softly.

Mama continued. "I didn't plan to be gone so long, but the Prices' baby fell ill and I couldn't leave that poor woman with a sick child and Grandpa."

Alice's face fell. Another flu victim. Mama looked into her

worried eyes. "It's not what you're thinking, Alice. The baby doesn't have the flu, just the sniffles. But sick babies take a lot of caring for and Mrs. Price was up with her several nights. She's doing much better now."

Alice breathed deeply. "That's a relief." She added, "Sick big sisters are a lot of work too."

"I imagine they are."

Alice shared her day with Mama.

"Alice made me drink baking soda," Ben piped up, interrupting the conversation. "It was yucky."

Father squeezed Ben's shoulder. "Good for her."

Mama's eyes grew large as Alice talked of Ellen's delirium. As if on cue, Ellen shrieked.

Her eyes were wide and again she was pointing at the empty, now darkened, window. She pedaled backwards until her knees were drawn up to her chest. She was a ball of fever and terror.

The family jumped into action as Ellen once again tried to bolt from the bed. As Father held her down, Mama stroked her thrashing head. Alice climbed into the other side of the bed and grabbed Ellen's hand as it flew through the air. As suddenly as it came, the fit was over and Ellen collapsed into exhausted sleep.

Thursday brought much the same. Friday was no better. Alice divided her time between caring for Ellen and keeping the house in order. When she wasn't feeding Ellen oniony chicken soup or whispering encouraging sister words in Ellen's ear, she was hanging out the clothes, doing the dishes, or scrubbing the floor with Ben's "help." Each night she collapsed into Paul's abandoned bed, fingering his newspaper birthday hat hung jauntily from the bed post, and saying a prayer for his safe return home.

Then she'd pray for Ellen. Ellen was alive, but very weak. If Ellen died, Alice didn't think she could go on.

Her final thoughts each night before she drifted into troubled sleep were of Alex. How she missed him. She longed to sit in her tree and talk with him for hours. She longed to kiss him again. Now she could hardly stand to go to her tree. Its bare limbs were missing more than leaves.

Saturday morning, Alice awoke early. Birds sang and Ben snored. The sun was turning the blackness of night into a fuzzy, dim brown. She tried to go back to sleep, but the racket inside and outside the room was too much. She padded softly across the creaking floorboards to Ellen's sickroom.

Days earlier, Father had carried Mama's rocking chair up to the room, and Mama sat, head on her shoulder, asleep. Days and nights of keeping vigil had been too tiring.

Alice tiptoed to the bed. She could just make out Ellen's still features in the predawn light.

# Chapter Twenty-five

Alarm shot through Alice's body like it had so many times as she watched over her sick and dying patients. Ellen was so still. Alice felt Ellen's cheek through the mask. Cool. A flutter of butterflies danced in her stomach. Had Ellen's fever broken—or had she died quietly during the night?

Ellen answered Alice's panicked thoughts by slowly opening her blue eyes. She whispered faintly, "Thank you."

Alice sat on the edge of the bed and took Ellen's frail hand. Relief flooded through her.

"You scared us."

"I scared myself...the family?"

"Everyone's fine. No one else has gotten sick."

"That's good."

Ellen's voice crackled and she seemed to be struggling to talk. Alice held Ellen's head up and helped her drink a glass of water.

The water helped. Ellen's voice was clearer. "I can't remember much. How long have I been sick?"

"You fell sick Wednesday. Today's Saturday."

"So many nightmares."

"You were delirious from the fever."

"Was Alex just a delirium?"

"No, Alex really died."

Ellen squeezed Alice's hand. "I was hoping I had dreamt it."

Darkness settled over Alice's heart. Would she ever be able to think about Alex again without her heart breaking?

"Alice, you took good care of me. Did you tell me you needed me to live?"

"Yes."

"I remember." Ellen's eyes fluttered closed.

Her blue eyes reopened and stared fixedly into Alice's. "You're a good sister."

"So are you." Alice wrapped her arms awkwardly around Ellen

and the layers of quilts and blankets. She kissed her cool forehead and stood.

Ellen's legs moved under the quilt. "I guess it's about time to make breakfast." She started to sit up, then fell back onto the bed.

"Not for you. I have a feeling you'll be resting up for a long time."

Alice's words proved true. Ellen gained strength every day, but was still in bed a week later. The sisters talked and talked, making up for years of silence. Alice finally found out why Ellen had been so afraid of the influenza.

Ellen had become seriously ill with pneumonia when she was five years old. The struggle to breathe, deep coughing that shook her tiny body, and adults' quiet, nervous whispers had terrified her. The memories haunted her still. She had been in bed for weeks. Alice asked question after question, trying to better understand how Ellen had felt as a scared, sick little girl. And how Alex had probably felt just days ago. Alice hadn't even remembered Ellen being that sick, because she had been only three at the time. It was strange that she lived in the same house with Ellen, shared a room with her, and had never really known her.

Ellen learned about Alice, too. One particularly exhausting afternoon, Alice brought yet another bowl of oniony chicken soup to Ellen and laid the tray across her lap. She plopped onto the bed next to Ellen to take a break, jostling some of the soup out of the bowl.

"Careful!"

"Sorry." Alice stared at the ceiling, wishing things could go back to normal.

"Thinking about Alex?"

Alice sighed. "Yes, I miss him so much."

"Talk about him," Ellen urged quietly. "Tell me all the good things you remember about Alex. Everything. Maybe it will help a little."

Alice put her hands behind her head and sunk into the pillow. "I like his eyes...*liked* his eyes." She trailed off. The room was blurring. She blinked back tears.

"You can say like. Alex is still alive inside your heart. He lives in all of us who knew him." Ellen gently turned Alice's face to her own. "What else do you like?"

"I like—I like the way he acts with Anna and Caleb—like a little kid...and he doesn't squish spiders—he puts them outside...and he's afraid of roller coasters. Did I ever tell you about the Dip the Dips?"

"Tell me."

All Alice's memories of Alex flooded her mind and heart and spilled out her lips. It was if Alex were alive, in the room with them, giving Caleb piggy back rides, building carousels with his erector set, sitting with Alice in her tree.

"He kissed me," Alice blurted out as that scene filled her mind. "In my tree."

"Alice!" Ellen had begun in an alarmed voice, then paused and calmly continued. "In our own backyard? What was it like?"

"I don't know!" Alice said, sitting up. "You know..."

"No, I don't," Ellen confessed.

"Of course you do. Lots of boys have come calling on you. You sit on the porch with them for hours. You're telling me you've never been kissed by any of them?"

"I've seen you peeking through the curtains at us. Have you ever seen a boy kiss me?"

"No, but I just figured I missed the good part."

Ellen put her hands on her hips, nearly tipping her tray. "Ha, ha." She admitted quietly, "Actually, they've asked, but I've been waiting for someone special. You know, like Alex is special to you..."

Alice and Ellen grew closer than they had ever been. Still, they quarreled some. Ellen was still bossy, even from her sick bed. And Alice preferred to hurry through her work rather than do a perfect job, which seemed to irritate Ellen to no end. But each time they'd make up and in no time they were planning a new dress for Ellen or talking about kids from school. Life went on, but Alex left an unfillable hole.

Alice had kept writing to Paul. After much debate with herself she had told Paul about Alex. Tears had smeared the ink, causing Alice to rewrite the horrid words several times until they were legible. Alex himself had convinced her that Paul needed to know what was really going on. *He needs to know. I would want to know...* Alex had told her after Vivien's death. Paul deserved the truth.

Now, at least she had some good news to report. The flu epidemic was slowing down its march over humanity, around Cincinnati and other cities. Right next door, the Longwells were on the mend. As Alice read to Ben on the porch one afternoon Mrs. Longwell stopped over, Anna and Caleb in tow. As Mrs. Longwell thanked Alice for all her help, Anna handed Alice a picture she had colored.

"For Paul."

"I'll send it with my letter this afternoon," Alice said, admiring the drawing.

"I colored my best, but Caleb wrecked it," Anna reported pointing at scribbles adorning the edge. She turned to glare at Caleb who was poking at an ant on the porch with a stubby finger.

"I think it's beautiful, Anna," Alice said.


Alice's letters to Paul were getting quite lengthy between Anna's artwork and Grandpa's occasional scrawled pages. After several days on his own trying to care for himself and a couple near accidents on the way to the water closet, Grandpa had been convinced to move in with the family until his leg healed. Taking Grandpa on the dreaded trolley with his broken leg had been a harrowing experience for all involved. But now that Grandpa was settled into Mama and Father's bedroom, he seemed to be in less pain and was almost back to his cantankerous self.

As the calendar flipped from October to November, one subject the family never tired of was the war. Alice had hated listening to her father read the casualty lists and war news before, but now the news was good. Austria had surrendered November 4th, followed a couple days later by Germany. The war was ending! That meant Paul would be coming home! Alice and Ellen made plans for a party in his honor.

"We can have meatloaf and baked potatoes—his favorites," suggested Ellen.

"And I'll make him a new hat out of newspaper that says

*Germany Surrenders.*"

"Isn't he kind of old for a paper hat?"

"He liked his birthday hat," Alice insisted.

"Fine. You can make him a hat. I'll knit him a sweater to keep him warm all winter."

"Go ahead. I hate knitting. All that counting." She made a face, then walked to the window and pushed the curtains back to let the budding sunlight in. "I wish Paul was coming home in time for the big celebration tomorrow. The signing of the peace treaty!"

"Me, too. I guess it takes time to get everyone back home."

# Chapter Twenty-six

November 11th dawned cool and sunny. Alice awoke full of anticipation. At first she couldn't remember why she was so excited. It wasn't Christmas. Or her birthday. Suddenly, she remembered. The War to End All Wars was over! There would be peace.

Alice found it hard to remember a time when people weren't buying war bonds and the newspaper didn't list the casualties every day. She leaped out of bed. Hurrying to dress, she shivered as the cold, peachy cloth of her favorite dress enveloped her body. A vigorous rubbing of arms and legs warmed her slightly. She gathered Alex's last note from the dresser, read it for the hundredth time, and slipped it into her pocket as she had each day since finding it. The edges were growing fuzzy from being in her dress pocket, but somehow she felt better with this little piece of Alex with her. She tied a matching bow into her hair, then dashed back to the bed.

"Ellen! Wake up!"

Ellen's eyes flittered open. Though weak, Ellen had improved dramatically over the past week and a half.

"What is it?"

"It's here! The war's over!"

"Help me get dressed."

"Are you sure?" Alice asked.

"Positive. I'm not missing this."

Digging through Ellen's drawers, Alice scrounged for each item Ellen requested.

"Not my blue checkered dress, my blue satin."

"Why do you have two blue dresses anyway?" Alice asked, anxious to get on with the dressing and get downstairs. "You have twice the number of clothes I do."

"I do not. And if I do have more it's because yours have been torn to shreds on tree branches and creek rocks. Now I wanted my petticoat with the ruffles, not the plain."

"Do you want my help or not? I could go downstairs without you and leave you stranded," Alice warned, half kidding, half serious.

"Sorry. I just want to look my best. It's the first time I'll be out of bed in weeks."

"And Clarence Spencer might pass by." Ellen blushed. Alice had learned all kinds of things about Ellen over the past weeks, including that she had a crush on Clarence Spencer, a boy in her class who lived down the street.

When Ellen was dressed to her satisfaction, Alice gave her an arm for support and helped her out of the room and down to the parlor. The trek took ten solid minutes and Alice began to think she'd spend this momentous day standing on the stairs. She was sure she'd have a bruised arm where Ellen clung with a surprisingly strong, if shaky hand.

As the family hurried through breakfast, gunshots rang out. Amidst Father's protests Alice dashed off her chair, through the parlor, and out the front door. Clarence Spencer and a couple friends were hooting and jogging through the streets. Clarence shot off another round into the air, did an impromptu dance, and continued down the road. Boy would Ellen have her hands full if she caught that one.

All down the street neighbors who had locked themselves away from the world for weeks were standing on porches, sitting on chairs on their lawns, chatting over fences. American flags decorated every porch. An all-American party in every way—except one. Every face was protected by a white mask, from old Mr. Schneider across the street to little Caleb Longwell. Even Alice donned the silly thing, because Mama insisted. Soon that too would come to an end, just as the war had.

Anna darted across her yard to Alice, waving a small American flag in each fist. Caleb toddled behind. Meeting the children in the grass, she stooped to give each a big hug. Mrs. Longwell followed her wandering offspring. Anna waved one of her flags in Alice's face, then handed it to her.

"I hear school's starting up again," Mrs. Longwell said.

"In two days."

"Looking forward to it?"

"I never thought I'd say this, but, yes." And she really meant it. She couldn't wait for things to return to normal. At least partly normal.

Alice felt a tug on her dress. Caleb looked up at her. "Pony wide! Alex!"

A lump instantly filled Alice's throat and she couldn't talk.

Mrs. Longwell quickly lifted Caleb to her hip. "Not now, Honey." She smoothed her son's golden locks and looked sadly at Alice.

Bells began their melodious clamor from the church.

"Church bells, Mama!" squealed Anna and started to run toward the peals. "Bye, Alice!"

Caleb squirmed to be put down. Once again the Longwell parade of three was off, running, followed by waddling, followed by walking.

Alice turned to the Becks' porch. Most of the festive mood had missed their home. Mr. Beck stood on crutches, one pants leg pinned up at the knee. Alice hadn't seen him since he had arrived home, days too late to see his son alive a final time. He looked so thin. And sad. Mrs. Beck's expression, as she stood by his side, was a mirror of her husband's. The war was over. The flu epidemic was ending. But this tiny family would never be the same again.

Alice forced her legs to walk toward the Becks' porch, as her mind sought frantically for comforting words. She reached the Becks' before words came, but words no longer seemed important. She scrambled up the steps and threw her arms around Mrs. Beck. Alice felt Mr. Beck's warm arm around her shoulder as he joined the hug.

Alice felt some peace, encircled by Alex's parents. These people shared her pain and loss. They loved Alex as much as she did. More.

Like Alex's parents, Alice would never be the same. A piece of her heart would always be for Alex. But she had to go on. For Alex. For herself. She had promised him.

Maybe they could help each other through this pain. She could share Alex's last letter with them. She felt the stiffness of Alex's note in her pocket, but left it inside. Maybe, someday. But not today. The hug was enough for now.

Alice stepped back and gave each grieving parent a half smile. She stepped slowly down the steps and through the soft grass, to her own yard.

Returning home, Alice found her family on the porch. Ben held an oatmeal muffin carefully in a napkin. His mask was on top of his head like a hat so his mouth would be free to eat. Father was receiving his own arm bruises as he helped Ellen to the porch swing. Grandpa sat in Father's arm chair just inside the front door while Mama draped a quilt over his propped leg.

Only Paul was missing, but he'd be home soon.

Alice waved Anna's borrowed flag high and joined her family on the porch to celebrate peace.

# Facts about the Spanish Influenza Pandemic of 1918

The Spanish Influenza Pandemic (an epidemic which affects the whole world) killed more people than World War I. In 1918 in ten months' time 675,000 Americans died from this killer disease. Hundreds of thousands died all over the world. The flu spread quickly because no one knew what caused it. Years later scientists discovered bacteria and found out that it spreads from person to person like a cold. The masks that Ellen and others relied on did little or no good against so tiny an attacker. People swore that certain remedies like kerosene, baking soda, or onions helped cure the influenza, but scientists are still not sure today why some people exposed to the flu died, like Alex, while others did not even fall ill, like Alice. This disease was unusual because most of the people who died from it were young people—teenagers to adults in their thirties. It was said that people would feel fine in the morning and die that evening. Influenza strains are seldom this deadly. Cities like Cincinnati fared better than others because they closed schools and other public places quickly once influenza cases were diagnosed. People didn't have as much contact with each other so the disease couldn't spread as quickly. Other cities like Philadelphia and San Francisco, which were attacked by the disease earlier in the year, lost many more people because schools remained open and people gathered in large crowds for War Bond parades. Army camps were filled with flu because the men were in such cramped quarters the disease spread quickly from person to person.

Printed in the United States
17669LVS00001B/106-123